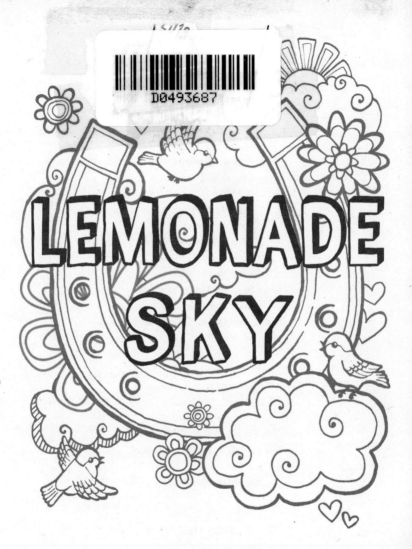

LEMONADE SKY

LEMONADE SKY

Jean Ure

HarperCollins *Children's Books*

First published in Great Britain by HarperCollins *Children's Books* in 2012
HarperCollins *Children's Books* is a division of HarperCollins*Publishers* Ltd, 77-85
Fulham Palace Road, Hammersmith, London, W6 8JB.

www.harpercollins.co.uk

www.jeanure.com

1

Lemonade Sky
Text © Jean Ure 2012
Illustrations © HarperCollins *Publishers* 2012

The author and illustrator assert the moral right to be
identified as the author and illustrator of this work.

ISBN 978-0-00-743164-9

Printed and bound in England by
Clays Ltd, St Ives plc.

CHAPTER ONE

As soon as I opened my eyes, I knew that something was wrong. When you live in a basement it is always a bit gloomy, but I could tell from the way the sun was shining through the tops of the windows that it had to be late.

I lay for a moment, watching the dust specks

dancing in the light. Where was Mum? Why hadn't she woken us?

From across the room there came the sound of gentle snoring. Either Tizz or Sammy, whiffling in her sleep. I raised myself on an elbow and gazed across at them. Tizz, in the top bunk, was lying on her back with her arms outside the duvet. Sammy was scrunched in a heap, sucking at her thumb. She was the one that was whiffling. Little snuffly noises, like a piglet.

Somewhere outside, further up the road, a church clock was striking. I sank back down, counting the bongs. Ten o'clock! If Mum was awake, she'd have come crashing in on us hours ago.

"Up, up! Glorious sunshine! Don't waste it! Out you get!"

I strained my ears, listening for some sign of movement. Anything to indicate that Mum was up and about. All I could hear was Sammy, whiffling, and the occasional sound of a car going past.

I pulled the duvet up to my chin. There wasn't any

actual need to get up; it wasn't like it was a school day. Sometimes at weekends, if Mum was in one of her depressed moods, she'd let us go on sleeping cos she'd be sleeping herself. But just lately she'd been on a high. What we called *a big happy*. When Mum was in a big happy she'd be up half the night, chatting on the phone to her friends, rearranging the furniture, even painting the walls a funny colour, which is what she did one time. We woke up to discover she'd painted the living room bright purple while we were asleep! Another time she'd spent the night baking things. The kitchen looked like a hurricane had blown through it. The sink was full of pots and pans, and everything was covered in flour. But Mum was so pleased with herself!

"See?" she said. "I've been cooking. Just like a real mum!"

I didn't have the heart to tell her that the lovely cake she'd made tasted like lumpy porridge. Sammy spat it out, but Tizz and me were brave and forced ourselves to swallow it. After all, Mum had been up half the night making it for us. It would have hurt her if we hadn't eaten it.

Even at weekends, she still got up at the crack of dawn. When she was in one of her big happies she didn't seem to need very much sleep. We'd hear her, at six o'clock in the morning, dancing round the sitting room, playing music, or just clattering pans in the kitchen.

This morning, there was silence. Nothing but the sound of passing cars, and Sammy, snuffling. That's how I knew that something was wrong.

I slipped out of bed and crept through to Mum's room. I thought the worst would be that I'd find her asleep, which would mean she'd come out of her big happy and slipped into one of her depressions, and then I'd have to decide whether to shake her awake or just leave her. I wasn't ever sure which it was best to do. But Mum's bed was empty. It was difficult to tell whether she'd slept in it or not. The pillow was crumpled, and the duvet was thrown back, but that wasn't anything to go by. Mum never bothered much with bed-making or housework. Either she was in one of her big happies, which meant she had more exciting things to do; or else she was depressed, in which case she didn't have the energy. There were the odd moments in between, but not very many. Mostly she was either up or down.

I felt the sheet to see if it was warm, but it wasn't. It was quite cold. My stomach did this churning thing. *Where was Mum?* I rushed through to the sitting room, burst into the kitchen, threw open the bathroom door. There wasn't a sign of her. Not anywhere.

I shouted, *"MUM?"*

I don't know why I shouted. All it did was wake up Tizz and Sammy. They appeared at the door together, in their nightdresses, Sammy still sucking her thumb. Tizz said, "What's going on? Where's Mum?"

I shook my head. "I dunno. She's not here."

"So where is she?"

"I said, I don't know!"

"She's prob'ly still asleep."

"She's not," I said. "I've looked."

"*So where is she?*"

I could hear the note of panic in Tizz's voice. I knew that we were both remembering the last time this had happened, when we'd woken up to find Mum gone.

Sammy took her thumb out of her mouth. "Who's going to get breakfast?"

Tizz snapped, "Shut up about breakfast! This is serious."

It wasn't fair to turn on Sammy. She was only little. Not quite six, which was far too young to have anything more than vague memories of that other time. Just a baby, really. Eighteen months, that's all she'd been. I'd been eight, and Tizz had been the age Sammy was now. We could remember all too clearly.

"Maybe—" With a look of fierce determination, Tizz strode across to the door. "Maybe she's gone to see Her Upstairs."

"No! Tizz! Don't!" I yelled at her, and she stopped.

"I'm only going to check whether she's there."

"But s'ppose she isn't?"

Tizz bit her lip. She knew what I was thinking. Her Upstairs was a busybody at the best of times. She'd immediately want to know what was going on and why it was we were looking for Mum.

Tizz turned, reluctantly, and came back into the room. "She could just have gone up the shops."

"She wouldn't go without telling us."

"She might. Let's get dressed and go up there!"

Mum wasn't up the shops. Well, shop, actually. There's only the one she'd go to and that was the newsagent on the corner, where sometimes she'd send us for the odd carton of milk or loaf of bread if we ran out. But she wasn't in there and after what had happened last time we knew better than to ask if anyone had seen her. If Mum had gone missing, we mustn't let on. We left the shop, quickly, before we could draw attention to ourselves.

"She might have wanted something they didn't have and gone on to Tesco" said Tizz.

★ 11 ☆

"It's Sunday," I said. "Tesco wouldn't have been open yet."

Tizz said, "No, but you know what Mum's like. She doesn't always remember which day it is."

I didn't say anything to that. Tizz was just clutching at straws. She knew Mum hadn't gone to Tesco.

Sammy was growing more and more agitated. She kept tugging at my sleeve and going, "Ruby, ask! *Ask*, Ruby!"

I hesitated. Mr and Mrs Petrides, who own the shop, aren't as nosy as Her Upstairs. Maybe we *could* try asking if Mum had been in.

Tizz said, "No!" She obviously knew what I was thinking. "We don't tell *anybody*."

"Why not?" wailed Sammy. "Why can't we?"

"Because we can't," I said. "Let's just go home."

We trailed back up the road, and down the basement steps. I think both me and Tizz were hoping that Mum might have come back while we were out, but there still wasn't any sign of her. Sammy was starting to grizzle and complain that she was hungry. I tried to be patient with her cos I realised she was probably getting a bit frightened. Mum hadn't just gone out, she simply wasn't there.

It was Tizz, with her sharp eyes, who noticed the red light blinking on the telephone.

"There's a message!"

She swooped on it. Immediately, Mum's voice came swirling into the room.

"Darlings, darlings! Love you, darlings! Thinking of you! Always thinking of you! Don't worry, my darlings! We'll have lemonade sky! Lemonade sky! I promise you, poppets! That's what we'll have! Lemonade sky! Oh, darlings, such fun! Such fun it will be! Kissy kissy, mwah, mwah! Love you, darlings! Love you to bits! Always, always! Take care, my precious angels! Mummy loves you! Lemonade sky, don't forget!"

My heart sank as I listened. This was how it had been before. Mum talking at a hundred miles an hour, not making any sense. I could remember her taking us to school, pushing Sammy in her buggy, calling after us as we went through the gates, "Love you, darlings! Love you, love you!" All the other kids had turned to look, and me and Tizz had been embarrassed. Then when school let out that afternoon Mum hadn't been there, and we'd had to make our own way home. We'd found her whirling round the room, with Sammy in her arms, both of them made up with bright red lipstick and green eye shadow. She was whirling so fast that Sammy was growing scared and was starting to cry. We were quite scared, too. We'd begged and begged Mum to stop, but it seemed like she couldn't. In the end she'd let us take Sammy and we'd shut ourselves in our bedroom, not knowing what to do. Hours later, when we'd crept back out, Mum had disappeared. Now it was happening all over again.

Me and Tizz stood, helplessly, looking at each other.

"Was that Mum talking?" said Sammy.

I said, "Yes, that was Mum."

"Why's she sound all funny?"

"She's just being happy," said Tizz.

"'bout what?"

"I don't know! Cos she's enjoying herself."

"Sounds like she was in a club," I said. "All that noise in the background."

"So when did she ring?"

"Dunno." I pressed the red button on the phone. We listened again to Mum's voice, spilling excitedly into the room.

"Take care, my precious angels! Mummy loves you! Lemonade sky, don't forget!"

"What's lemonade pie?" said Sammy.

"*Sky*," said Tizz. "Just be quiet!"

The mechanical answerphone voice took over to tell us that that was the final message: "Sunday, 2.15 am."

"*Oh*," I said. "I thought I heard the phone ring!"

"So why didn't you answer it?" screamed Tizz.

"Cos I fell asleep again. Anyway, I thought Mum was here. I thought she'd answer it."

"Is it something to eat?" said Sammy.

We both turned on her. "Is what something to eat?"

"Lemonade pie."

"*Sky*," said Tizz. "Sky, sky, *sky!*"

"What's lemonade sky?"

"How should I know?" Tizz sounded exasperated. "Let's ring her back!"

We tried, but all we got was voice-mail. Either Mum had switched her phone off, or, most likely, she had run out of credit. She was always forgetting to top up.

"Maybe it's a treat," said Sammy. She looked at us, hopefully. "Mum's gone out to buy us a treat! For my birthday," she added. "It could be my birthday present!"

I said, "Maybe. Who knows?"

"Cos next week," said Sammy, "I'm going to be six."

"You are," I said. "It's a big age."

"When will she come back with it?"

"Soon," I said. It had been ten days, last time. Mum had been away for ten whole days! *But she had come back*. That was what we had to hold on to. Plus she had rung and left a message. She hadn't done that last time.

I said this to Tizz.

"But it's just babble," said Tizz. "It doesn't make any sense!"

"That's cos she's confused." It was what had happened before. Mum had become so hyper that her brain had run out of control. She'd told us, later, that she couldn't remember anything about where she'd been or what she'd done.

"I was just buzzing with all this energy, you know? Like my head was full of bees."

"At least this time," I said, "we know she's thinking about us."

Tizz said, "Huh!"

She didn't say it in her usual scoffing Tizz-like fashion. I had this feeling she was desperately trying not to show that she was every bit as scared as Sammy. I was scared, too, and I was desperately trying not to show it. With Tizz it was a matter of pride. Nothing frightens

Tizz! With me it was more like one of us had to stay on top of things, and as I was the oldest, I didn't really have much choice.

"We should have known," said Tizz.

She meant we should have known that Mum was in danger of going over the edge. She'd been wound up, tight as a coiled spring, for days. She's OK if she takes her meds, but sometimes she forgets. Or sometimes she doesn't take them cos she reckons she can do without. It's up to us to keep an eye on her. She's our mum, we're supposed to look after her.

I said, "Omigod!"

I raced through to the bathroom and flung open the door of the bathroom cabinet. There, on the shelf, were Mum's pills. My heart went into overdrive, thumping and banging in my chest.

"What is it?" Tizz and Sammy had followed me in. Tizz peered over my shoulder.

"Mum's pills." I held up the bottle. "She's gone off without them!"

"Gimme!" Tizz wrenched the bottle away and wrestled with the top. I watched her with growing impatience.

"Here!" I snatched it back. "Let me." It was supposed to be child proof, but I knew how to open it. Tizz was too impatient. I got the top off and stared in dismay. The bottle was full! I held it out to show Tizz. Her little pinched face turned pale beneath its freckles. We both knew that Mum had got a new prescription from the doctor over a month ago.

"She hasn't been taking them," I whispered.

There was a long silence, broken only by a plaintive wail from Sammy, "I want my breakfast! I'm hungry!"

"Oh, will you just SHUT UP!" screeched Tizz. "Don't be so selfish all the time!"

Sammy's face crumpled. Tears welled into her eyes. I screwed the cap back on Mum's pills and shut the bottle away again in the cabinet. Then I sat on the edge of the bath and pulled Sammy into my arms.

"Don't cry," I said. "It'll be OK. I'll take care of us!"

"It's all very well *saying* that," said Tizz. "We don't even know if—"

"Stop it!" I begged. "*Please!*" I took a breath, trying to make myself be calm. "Mum *will* come back. She came back last time, she'll come back this time. But one thing we've not got to do, and that's fight!" I wiped Sammy's eyes with the edge of my T-shirt. "We'll be all right," I said, "so long as we look out for each other."

CHAPTER TWO

"What's important," I said, "is keeping things normal."

"*Normal?*" Tizz gave me this look, like, *are you out of your mind?* "How can things be normal, without Mum?"

"Normal as possible," I said. "For Sammy."

I'd sent her off to watch telly while I rooted

about in the kitchen to see what I could find for breakfast. There had to be something! But there wasn't.

"I don't believe this," I said.

Tizz said, "*What?*" in this rather grumpy tone.

"There's nothing in the fridge!"

Grudgingly, she came over to look.

"What's that?" She pointed to a carton of milk. I picked it up and shook it.

"It's empty, practically. And there's only a tiny bit of butter, and the bread's almost gone."

Tizz marched across to a cupboard and yanked it open.

"*Cereal.*" She banged the packet down on the table. "*Marmalade.*"

But the cereal packet was only a quarter full, and the marmalade jar, like the fridge, was almost empty. When Mum stopped taking her meds, she didn't always notice that the cupboards were getting bare. Just like she didn't sleep much, she didn't eat much, either. If she'd been at home she'd have sent us up the road to the corner shop.

Me and Tizz stood, looking at each other. I knew that we were both thinking the same thing: how were we going to feed ourselves?

Tizz ran her fingers through her hair, sticking it up on end.

"D'you think she's left any money?"

"Dunno." I picked up the cereal packet and shook it, helplessly. "Let's at least give Sammy something to eat."

Well! We ran into trouble straight away. Sammy didn't want cereal, she wanted a boiled egg.

"Bald egg and fingers!"

When I said we didn't have any eggs and she should just eat what she was given, she complained because there wasn't any juice.

"Mum gives me juice!"

We didn't have any juice. I found a tiny dribble of squash, which I made up for her, but she spat it out, saying it was watery.

"Just think yourself lucky you've got anything at all," scolded Tizz. "We haven't got anything."

Only tea bags, and we both hate tea. 'Specially without milk. We had to keep the milk to go with the cereal. There was just enough for Tizz and Sammy, but then we couldn't find any sugar, so that got Sammy going again.

"I can't eat Krispies without sugar!"

Tizz said, "Oh, for goodness' sake!" She picked up the marmalade jar, spooned out a dollop and dumped it on top of Sammy's bowl.

"There! Stir that in."

"It's marm'lade," whined Sammy. "I don't like marm'lade!"

"Just get on with it," snarled Tizz.

Sniffling, Sammy did so.

There were five slices of bread in the bin, but they were all hard, so I had to toast them.

"You have two," said Tizz, "cos you didn't have any cereal."

And now there wasn't any marmalade left, which meant I had to eat toast and marge, which is horrible, but there was only a scraping of butter and I let Sammy have that cos she won't eat marge at any price.

"Call this normal?" said Tizz, pulling a face.

"We'll go up the road," I said. "After breakfast. We'll buy stuff."

"What with?"

"Money!" chortled Sammy. I guess she thought it was a joke.

"Yeah, right," said Tizz. "Money."

I jumped up. "Let's look first and check what's in the cupboard." There *might* just be enough to keep us going.

I pulled out everything I could find and stacked it up on the table. There wasn't very much. A tin of baked beans, a tin of spaghetti, two tins of tomato soup, a tin of sausages and a tin of pilchards.

We sat there, staring at them.

"That's not going to last ten days," said Tizz. "Not even if we just have one tin a day. *Between* us."

Sammy was looking worried. "Why's it got to last ten days?" Her lip wobbled. "When's Mum coming back?"

"Soon," I said, "soon! But just in case – I mean, just *in case* she's away for ten days–"

Ten days, like last time. Sammy's face crumpled.

"Where is she? Where's she gone?"

"See, we're not actually sure," I said. I said it as gently as I could, but there wasn't any point in lying to her. "You know how sometimes Mum gets a bit, like... excitable? Like when she's having one of her big happies?"

Sammy nodded, doubtfully, and stuck her thumb in her mouth.

"It can make her do things she wouldn't normally do. Like—"

"Disappearing," said Tizz.

"But it's all right," I said, quickly. "She'll come back! It's just that we have to take care of ourselves while she's not here.

"And not tell anyone that she's gone!"

I said, "Yes, we've not got to tell *anybody*. Not *anybody*."

That was the mistake we'd made last time. We'd been living over the other side of town, then, in an upstairs flat, and we'd been so scared when Mum went off that we'd told the lady in the flat next to ours, and she'd rung the Social Services people, and they'd come and taken us away. Even when Mum had turned up again they wouldn't let us go back to her. It had been months before they said she was well enough to take responsibility for us. And all that time me and Tizz had been in a children's home and Sammy had been with foster parents. That had been the worst part, being split up. We weren't going to let that happen again.

We'd still been quite little, then. Too young to look after ourselves. But I was twelve now, and Tizz was ten, and nobody, but nobody, was going to come and take us away!

"I don't suppose you remember last time?" said Tizz.

Slowly, Sammy shook her head.

"She was only a baby," I said. "But now she's big – she's nearly six! She can be trusted to keep a secret. Can't you?"

Sammy said, "What secret?"

"About Mum not being here. We don't want people knowing, cos if they know they'll put us in a home, they'll say we can't take care of ourselves. But we can," I said, "can't we?"

Sammy sucked on her thumb. She seemed uncertain.

"Of course we can!" I said. "We're not stupid. Just think how proud Mum will be when she gets back and we tell her all the things we've done!"

"Such as what?" said Tizz. "Eating toast and marge and Rice Krispies with marmalade?"

I scowled at her, over Sammy's head.

"I only *asked*," said Tizz.

I said, "Well, don't! Have a bit of imagination."

Tizz hunched a shoulder.

"Can we stay up late?" said Sammy. "And watch whatever we like on TV?"

"You've got it," said Tizz.

She really *wasn't* helping. I said, "Maybe just now and again. Not all the time, though, cos that wouldn't be right. Mum wouldn't like it if we did that."

"Will she be here for my birthday?"

"She might," I said. "But if not, we'll have a big bash when she gets back."

"Seems to me," said Tizz, "before we start thinking about birthdays we ought to find out if there's any money anywhere."

I knew that she was right. If we didn't have any money, I couldn't think what we would do.

First off, we looked in the saucer on the kitchen windowsill where Mum sometimes kept bits and pieces of change. There was a little bit in there. We set Sammy to counting it. Proudly she announced that it came to "£3 and 20p." Meanwhile, I had £2 in my purse, and Tizz produced a fiver. I said, "Wow!"

"I was *saving* it," said Tizz.

"That's all right," I said. "Mum'll give it back."

Tizz said, "You reckon?"

I think it must be dreadful to be so untrusting. But Tizz is one of those people, she has a very dim view of human nature. Even though she knows Mum can't *help* being sick, she gets impatient.

"Let's go through pockets," I said.

We went through all of Mum's pockets, and all of our own, but all we came up with was a 5p piece.

Tizz said, "Try down the side of the sofa. That's what they do in books. They always manage to find something."

We didn't find anything at all. Not unless you count an old button, plus a needle that stuck in my finger and made me yelp.

"Is that blood?" quavered Sammy.

Tizz said, "Yes, but it's not yours, so you don't have to start freaking out! Let's go and see if there's anything in Mum's secret stash."

She meant the old Smarties tube where Mum

sometimes hoarded 20p pieces. We raced through to Mum's bedroom and sure enough, in the top drawer of her dressing table, there was the Smarties tube and oh! Hooray! It had something in it.

We carried it through to the kitchen and upended it. 20p pieces rolled about the table. Greedily, we counted them off into piles.

"That's £4.60," said Tizz.

It did seem wrong to be taking Mum's money, especially when I had this unhappy feeling she'd probably been keeping it to buy something for Sammy's birthday, but it couldn't be helped.

"So how much have we got altogether?" I said. I waited for Tizz to add things up, cos she is good at arithmetic. She did some sums on a bit of paper.

"£14.75."

Sammy's face lit up. "That's a *lot*," she said.

It sounded like a lot. But was it? I wasn't sure. I realised that I simply didn't know. I had no idea what anything cost! When Mum sent us up the road it was usually just for bread, or milk, or maybe a tin of something. She'd give us a couple of pounds, and we'd hand it over and come back with the change, but I'd never properly bothered to count how *much* change. I'd always just accepted whatever Mrs Petrides gave us. It had never occurred to me to check prices. If Mum said buy a large loaf, I bought a large loaf. I picked it off the shelf and took it to the checkout and that was that.

I wished, now, that I'd paid a bit more attention.

Tizz was busy on another load of sums. She looked up and glared, fiercely, across the table.

"I don't *think*," she said, "that a person can live on 49p a day."

I said, "What are you talking about?"

"49p," said Tizz. "That's how much we'll each have to live on if Mum is away for ten days."

I looked at her, doubtfully. I wasn't sure what you could actually buy for 49p. Just bars of chocolate, maybe, or packets of crisps. But they weren't healthy! Even I knew that.

"We've got all this stuff," I said, pointing at the tins we'd taken out of the cupboard.

"Yeah." Tizz barely glanced at them. "That'll go a long way."

I did wish she would stop being so negative all the time. It really didn't help. I pointed out that people had been known to survive on nothing but bread and water for days on end.

"Just so long as you have enough to drink," I said. "That's the main thing."

"We'll starve," said Tizz.

"We won't starve!" Didn't she listen to a word I said? "Watch my lips: *we are not going to starve*. I won't let us!"

"Dunno what you think you're gonna do about it," said Tizz. She scrunched up the paper she'd been doing her sums on and hurled it savagely across the room. "Mum might at least have left us some money!"

I said, "She didn't know." It wasn't like Mum planned these things. She just got overwhelmed. "Anyway," I said, "after yesterday she probably doesn't *have* any money."

Yesterday had been such a good day. Mum's friend Nikki had come round with her boyfriend and we'd all gone off to the Carnival on the Common. It's held every year, but this was the first time we'd ever been. There were all kinds of stalls, where you could play Guess the Weight or have a lucky dip or throw hoop-las, and lots of different rides, some of them quite scary. Well, I found them scary! I am a bit of a cowardy custard like that. Tizz was eager to try everything, and Mum let her. Like she let Sammy have three goes at the lucky dip, until she managed to pick something she really wanted.

We were so busy enjoying ourselves we didn't ever stop to wonder where the money was coming from. Mum just kept laughing, and spending, and Nikki and her boyfriend kept saying, "Go for it!" Like egging her on. *Encouraging* her. Mum doesn't need encouragement! Not when she's all hyper. She needs someone to take charge and be responsible.

I should have taken charge. I should have been responsible. I knew Mum couldn't afford to pay for all those rides, and all those goes on the lucky dip. Plus we all had vegeburgers, and doughnuts, and fizzy drinks. *And* Mum paid for Nikki and her boyfriend. *And* they let her. Just taking advantage of Mum's good nature. They know when she's on a high she loses all control.

She'd gone off again, that evening, to meet them. She'd been in a mad whirl, all laughing and flying about from room to room, trying on clothes then tearing them off again.

"Darlings, how do I look? Do I look like a hag?"

Like she ever could! Mum is really pretty. Very slim and delicate, with big blue eyes and a foaming mass of hair, red as the setting sun.

"I feel haglike," she said. "I can't go out feeling haglike!"

How I wished, now, that she hadn't gone out. But we'd assured her she looked beautiful, and we'd even helped her, in the end, choose which clothes to wear.

She'd gone waltzing off, as happy as could be. But I couldn't help wondering how much money she'd had left. It couldn't have been very much; not after her mad spending spree. Almost nothing, I'd have thought. How was she going to manage, without any money?

Tizz could obviously sense what was going through my mind.

"It's that Nikki," she said. "She leads Mum astray."

"She's supposed to be Mum's friend," I said.

Tizz snorted. "Some friend!"

I wondered if Nikki knew that Mum hadn't come home. I couldn't ring her cos I didn't have her number. I didn't even know where she lived.

"Her and that stupid Zak." Tizz said it vengefully. "They're the ones that made Mum spend all her money!"

They certainly hadn't done anything to stop her. But then neither had I. On the other hand, even if I'd tried I doubt Mum would have taken any notice. She'd just have laughed and cried, "Oh, darling, don't be such a bore! You take life far too seriously. Try to have a bit of fun, for once."

I had had fun! It had been the best day I could remember for a long time. And now I was feeling guilty.

I thrust my hair back, behind my ears.

"We'll manage," I said. "Don't worry!" I leaned over and gave Sammy a hug. She had been listening, solemnly, darting anxious glances from one to the other of us. "What we have to do," I said, "is decide what's most important. Stuff we need to keep us going. Like bread, and milk, and stuff."

Sammy brightened. "Fishy fingers!"

"Chips," said Tizz.

I said, "Chips aren't good for you. We've got to have stuff that's healthy. Like pasta," I said. "That's supposed to be good for you."

Tizz pulled a face. "*Bo-ring!*"

"Doesn't matter if it's boring. You don't think when people go to the North Pole they worry about stuff being boring? They worry about what's good for them, like – I don't know! Dried fish, and stuff."

"You gotta be joking," said Tizz, "if you think we're going to eat dried fish!"

I could see that my task was not going to be easy. Tizz is just *so* difficult at times.

"Wait there," I said. I went back to the bedroom and dug a notebook out of my school bag. "Right!" I slapped it down on the table. Tizz eyed it suspiciously.

"What's that for?"

"We need to work things out," I said.

"You mean, you're going to get all bossy?"

I said, "Well, someone has to. Would you rather it was you?"

Tizz hunched a shoulder.

"You want to take over?" I pushed the pad towards her, but she shoved it back at me.

"I don't want it!"

I knew she wouldn't. The thing about Tizz, she may be sharp as needles and full of mouth, but she is far too impatient to ever sit down and actually plan anything. She also hates being told what to do. It is a constant battle! I know that I am not as bright as she is, but I do usually get things done in the end. Slow but sure, is what Mum says.

"OK!" I reached out for a pen. "We're going to sit here," I said, "and make a shopping list."

CHAPTER THREE

In the end, we made two lists. The first was things we
had to have:

Bread
Milk
Marge

Cheese

Eggs

Cereal

Mostly chosen by *me*.

The second was things we'd like to have:

Pizza

Fish Fingers

Chocolate Biscuits

Orange Squash

Sugar

Jam

Meatballs

All of them chosen by Tizz and Sammy.

"We'll have to go to Tesco," I said. "You can get stuff cheaper there."

Tizz didn't like that idea. She complained that it was a long way to walk and we'd have to carry heavy bags back with us. I told her that couldn't be helped.

"We've got to go where it's cheapest."

Tizz said, "That's not fair on Mr Petrides. He's a small shopkeeper. He has to be saved! It's people like you," said Tizz, "that put people like him out of business."

I did feel a slight twinge of guilt, cos in the past Mr and Mrs Petrides had been really good to us. Sometimes when Mum ran out of money they'd actually let us take stuff and pay for it later. You couldn't do that at Tesco. But I hardened my heart. I had to! It was a question of survival.

"I bet if we asked him," said Tizz, "he'd let us have things on tick."

On tick was what Mum called it when she couldn't afford to pay. I think maybe it meant that Mr Petrides put a tick by the side of her name in his account book.

"We'll only do that if we get desperate," I said. "Otherwise he might ask questions, like *where's your mum* or *why hasn't she been in?*"

"Mm… I s'ppose." Tizz said it reluctantly, but at least it stopped her arguing. The one thing we were terrified of was people asking questions. We'd be safe in Tesco cos nobody knew us.

I put all the money in my purse except for five £1 coins and five 20p pieces. Tizz watched, suspiciously.

"What are you doing with that lot?"

I said, "Saving it. I'm going to put *this* –" I scooped up the 20p pieces – "in here." I dropped them into the saucer that Mum kept on the windowsill. "They're in case we need a bit extra. And *this* –" the five pound coins – "is our emergency fund. I'm going to leave it indoors so we can't spend it. I'm going to hide it somewhere. Somewhere safe. Like…" I roamed about the kitchen, looking for a hiding place. "In with the flour!"

There was a half packet of flour in the cupboard, with an elastic band wrapped round it. I pushed the coins in there and put the flour back on the shelf.

Tizz said, "I bet that's the first place a burglar would think of looking."

I told her that I wasn't scared of burglars. "I'm scared of it getting lost."

"Like it absolutely would," said Tizz, "if it wasn't hidden in a bag of flour. I mean, if it was just put in an ordinary purse like any normal person would put it."

"I just don't want us being tempted into spending it," I said. "We've got to have something to fall back on."

Tizz said, "Yeah, like living on bread and marge. *Yuck!*"

Sammy said, "Ugh! Yuck! *Bluurgh.*"

They both bent over and pretended to be sick.

"We want chips," said Tizz. "We want pizza! We want—"

"Fishy fingers!"

"Yay!"

Tizz and Sammy smacked their hands together in a triumphant high five. I was glad that Sammy had cheered up, but I did hope we weren't going to have scenes in Tesco. I wasn't sure I could cope with that. It would be just so embarrassing! Everyone would look at us, especially if Sammy worked herself up into one of her states. Just now and again, if she can't get what she wants, she'll throw herself on the ground and drum her heels and refuse to get up. Mum is the only one who knows how to deal with her.

"*I* think," said Tizz, "if you want *my* opinion, we ought to be allowed to have whatever we want to have. Without you dictating to us!"

"Just buy *nice* things," said Sammy.

"Yeah! Right. 'Stead of all that boring muck!" Tizz waved a hand at my list of things we had to have.

I felt quite cross with her. She wasn't being at all helpful.

"Let's put down some other stuff." Tizz snatched up the second list and added CRISPS in big capital letters at the bottom of it.

"Sweeties!" shouted Sammy.

"SWEETIES," wrote Tizz.

She was being deliberately provoking. I almost felt like throwing my purse at her and telling her to get on with it. Let *her* take the responsibility. But of course she wouldn't; not when it came to it. She just wanted to challenge my authority. It is very difficult, sometimes, being the oldest, especially when you have a sister who refuses to do what she's told. *And* keeps getting the littlest one all worked up. I could see that Sammy was well on the way to having one of her screaming fits.

"Listen," I said. I squatted down beside her. Even a five-year-old can be made to see reason. "We'll try to buy *some* nice things, I promise you! But nice things are expensive and we can't afford too many of them, so—"

That was as far as I got because at that point someone hammered on the front door and we all froze. Well, me and Tizz froze. Sammy hesitated for just a second, then with a joyous cry of, "*Mum!*" went galloping off.

It wasn't Mum. It was Her Upstairs. Mrs Bagley. Mum calls her 'that woman'. We call her Her Upstairs. We don't like her.

She came pounding into the room with a scared-looking Sammy trailing behind her. She is such a huge great woman that the floor trembles as she walks.

"Where is your mother?" she said, in this big booming voice that practically made the walls shake.

I was about to say in quavering tones that Mum wasn't here when Tizz jumped in ahead of me.

"She's out," she said.

It is just as well that Tizz is so quick. The way she said it – "She's OUT" – was like, *what's it to do with you?* If I'd told her that Mum wasn't home, you can just bet she'd have demanded to know where she was, and then I wouldn't have known what to say. I don't think as fast as Tizz. She can always be relied on to come up with a smart answer.

Her Upstairs did this huffing thing. Sort of 'Pouf!' With her lips billowing out and her nostrils flaring, like she suspected Tizz of being impertinent. Tizz faced up to her, boldly.

"Can we give her a message?"

"You can indeed." Her Upstairs has these big bosoms. I mean, like, really really big. Like *massive*. Mum says you could lay a dinner table on them. When she gets indignant, which is what she was now, she kind of inflates them. I watched them heave and wondered what we'd done to upset her this time.

"You can tell your mother," she said, "that I have called for my flour."

I said, "F-flour?"

Even Tizz looked a bit taken aback. At any rate, she didn't say anything.

"My flour. My self-raising! I should like to have it back. If, of course –" her lip curled – "there is anything left to have back. Shall we go into the kitchen and see?"

She set off across the room. Thud, bang, stamp, across the floor. Tizz sprang into action.

"It's all right! Ruby'll get it for you."

"I will," I said. "I'll get it for you!"

I rushed into the kitchen, grabbed the bag of flour and scrabbled frantically in search of our pound coins.

I had to plunge my hand in so deep that great white clouds came puffing out all over me. And then, in my panic, I went and dropped the bag and loads of flour went and spilt over the floor.

But at least I had the coins! All five of them. I stuffed them into the back pocket of my jeans and wiped my top with the dish rag. Unfortunately, by now, there didn't seem to be very much flour left in the bag. Hardly any, in fact. Most of it was on the kitchen floor.

Hastily, I seized a tablespoon out of the drawer, scooped up as much as I could and poured it back into the bag. It probably wasn't very hygienic cos I didn't know when Mum had last had a cleaning session, but the way I saw it, flour was used for cooking and cooking killed germs. Anyhow, it was only Her Upstairs.

I went back into the sitting room. Her Upstairs was standing there, with her arms folded. Tizz was looking defiant. Sammy had rushed off to hide behind the sofa.

"I found it," I said. "There's still some left."

I held out the bag. Her Upstairs took it, rather grimly.

She removed the elastic band, looked in the bag and went, "Huh!" Then she looked at my top and went, "Hmph!"

"Mum *was* going to give it back," I said.

"Not before she managed to get through three quarters of it, I see. What on earth was she making?"

I looked helplessly at Tizz.

"Can't remember," said Tizz.

"I was under the impression she merely wanted a sprinkle. Perhaps you would be kind enough to inform her, when she gets back, that I should appreciate it, in future, if she would *not* come to me when she runs out of something."

"I will," I said. "I'll tell her."

"Thank you. I should be grateful."

Her Upstairs moved off, towards the door. I followed her, anxiously. Please, just let her *go.*

As she passed the table, where we'd laid out the stuff we'd found in the cupboard, she paused for a moment. I could almost hear her nosy parker brain ticking over.

What are they doing with all those tins? Where is their mother? What is going on?

It was Tizz, again, who came to the rescue.

"We're tidying up the cupboard," she said.

"Hm!" Her Upstairs gave a sniff. "Not before time, I dare say."

I resented that! It was criticism of Mum. Like saying she wasn't good at keeping things in order. Maybe she wasn't, but so what? She was our mum and we loved her! We didn't mind if the cupboards were in a mess. And what was it to do with Her Upstairs anyway?

"I hate that woman," said Tizz, when the door was safely closed.

I didn't like her very much either, especially when she was so mean about Mum, though I could sort of understand why she didn't want Mum asking for stuff any more. Cos I didn't think, really, that Mum *had* been going to give the flour back. Not that she would have kept it on purpose; just that it would have slipped her mind.

I said this to Tizz, but she got all angry and snapped, "Don't defend her, she's horrible! And you—" she whizzed round on Sammy, crawling out from behind the sofa. "Don't go running off to answer the door when you don't know who it is! You don't *want* us all to be split up, *do* you? Cos that's what'll happen if Her Upstairs finds out!"

Sammy's lower lip started to wobble. Tears came into her eyes. "I thought it was Mum!"

"If it had been Mum, she'd have used her key."

I thought, yes, if she hadn't lost it or had her bag stolen. I told Sammy to cheer up.

"We'll go shopping in a minute. That'll be fun!"

"Buy nice things?" said Sammy.

"We'll see."

"Fishy fingers!"

"Maybe."

Sammy glanced slyly at Tizz. "– Fishy fingers! We want fishy fingers!"

But Tizz wasn't playing any more. "Don't keep on," she said. "It's a question of what we can afford."

At last! She was beginning to give me some support. She didn't even grumble when I insisted on finding a new hiding place for our emergency fund.

"I'm just scared," I said, "that if we take it with us we might be tempted to spend it, and then we'll be left with nothing."

Tizz said, "Right."

"I mean, I know Mum *could* be back at any moment—"

She could! She really could! She could be there waiting for us when we got back from Tesco.

"It's just... you know! In case she isn't."

"This is it," said Tizz. "Got to be prepared."

Life was *so* much easier when Tizz decided to cooperate.

CHAPTER FOUR

"We've absolutely got to watch what we're spending," I said, as we wheeled our trolley into Tesco. It did make me feel a bit important, being in charge of the shopping. I told Tizz that she was to add things up as we went round.

"Make sure we don't overspend."

Tizz said, "OK."

"We've got £9.75. So when we get up to £9 you've got to let me know."

"OK," said Tizz.

We set off down the first aisle, heading for the bread counter. We'd been to Tesco loads of times with Mum, which was just as well cos otherwise it would have been really confusing. I picked up two large loaves and put them in the trolley.

"That's two at 55p," I said.

"Got it," said Tizz.

Sammy's hand was already reaching out towards the cakes. She likes the little squishy ones covered in green and pink goo. Mum sometimes lets her have one as a treat.

"*Rubeee!*" She tugged at my arm. "Cakies!"

"Not now," I said.

"Mum would let me!"

"Mum's not here," said Tizz.

"And anyway," I said, "they're not good for you."

Sammy's face crumpled. A woman walking past smiled, sympathetically.

"They are nice, though," she said, "aren't they?"

Well! *That* wasn't a very helpful remark. I hastily hauled Sammy off towards the milk and eggs. I reached out for two cartons of milk and stared in outrage.

"*£1.18?*" Just for a carton of milk?

"That's £3.36," said Tizz.

"Just for *milk?*"

Tizz shrugged.

"That'll only leave us…" I did some frantic finger work.

"£6.39," said Tizz.

I was beginning to understand how it was that Mum kept running out of money and having to buy things on tick and borrow stuff from Her Upstairs. Rather grimly, I marched on down the aisle.

"*Marge.*"

Sammy opened her mouth and let out a wail. "Don't like marge!"

"Nobody does," said Tizz. "We've all just got to put up with it."

I was so thankful that Tizz was being supportive at last. It was like the reality of the situation had suddenly hit her. Mum had disappeared and we were on our own. And if we didn't want to be split up, we had to learn how to take care of ourselves. It wasn't any use splurging on pink cakes and chocolate biscuits, then being forced to throw ourselves on the mercy of Her Upstairs cos we'd run out of money and there wasn't any food left.

"Let's get some eggs," I said.

I hadn't the least idea how much eggs cost. I thought maybe you might be able to get six for about 60p. I mean, 10p an egg seemed reasonable. They are only tiny. My mouth fell open when I saw that even the tiniest ones were £1.38 a carton.

"What'll we do?" I whispered. "We've got to have eggs!"

"We'll just get six," said Tizz. "If we have any money left we can always come back and get more."

I nodded, gratefully. It was such a relief to have someone else share the burden. "How much have we spent now?"

Tizz cast her eye over the contents of the trolley. I could almost see her brain whirring into action. "£5.53."

I do honestly think she is some kind of mathematical genius. She can do all these things in her head! "How much does that leave us?"

"£4.22."

I gulped. We hadn't even finished buying everything on list number one! We still had cheese and cereal to get.

We found some cheese triangles, which met with Sammy's approval, and a cheap bumper packet of Cornflakes, which didn't. She wanted Coco Pops or Sugar Puffs and couldn't understand why she couldn't have them.

"Thing is," said Tizz, "she's never going to eat Cornflakes without sugar."

I was tempted to say, "You mean, you're not," but that would have been unfair when Tizz was behaving so nicely.

I said, "I know what we'll do! We'll get some jam. That'll do instead of sugar, and then we can use it on bread as well."

Tizz looked doubtful, but she didn't argue. I had never known her so meek. It was actually a bit unsettling cos I knew it meant that she was worried.

We found some strawberry jam, and put it in the trolley. I was starting to feel important again. We were doing well!

"What's that leave us?"

"£2.44," said Tizz.

"Hm!" Perhaps, I thought, we should look at the second list and decide what was priority and what wasn't. We stood in a huddle by a freezer cabinet. "So what do you reckon?" I said.

We all had different ideas. I guess it was inevitable. Tizz wanted pizza, I said meatballs, Sammy shouted out

"Fishy Fingers!" at the top of her voice. "Fishy Fingers and choc'lit bikkies!"

"That's two things," said Tizz. "Just choose one."

But Sammy couldn't cope with that. She put a finger in her mouth and scowled.

"Let's go and check prices," I said.

Pizza was ruled out straightaway. We simply didn't have enough money left. We went for two tins of meatballs in the end, cos they were cheap. Like *really* cheap. I was impressed by how cheap! You could practically live on meatballs. We got a packet of fish fingers, cos it seemed only fair Sammy should have something she wanted, and that left us with exactly £1.

"What about orange squash?" said Tizz. "We ought to have something to drink."

I mumbled, "Water," but Tizz had found a whole big bottle of squash for only 99p so it was really hard to say no, especially as I'd got my meatballs and Sammy had her fish fingers and Tizz, so far, didn't have anything. She was behaving *so* well!

"Can we?" she said, waving the bottle at me.

I said, "Yes, all right. Let's go and pay."

Standing in front of us at the checkout was a family. A mum and a dad and two children. One of the children was perched in the seat at the back of the trolley. The other, a little boy about Sammy's age, was clutching a packet of sweets he'd grabbed from a display stand. His mum said, "What are you doing with that? Put it back!" She tried to take it off him, but he gave this naughty grin and clutched it even tighter. He obviously knew his mum was a soft touch. She not only let him have the sweets but even told him to pick something up for his sister. His dad said, "That boy twists you right round his little finger," but you could tell he wasn't really bothered. I thought that those two children were well spoilt. I couldn't help wishing we had a dad that came shopping with us and let us pick up bags of sweets.

Sammy, of course, had seen it all going on and was reaching out *her* hand to grab something.

"Sammy, don't!" I said.

"I want one," said Sammy. "I want a bag of sweeties!"

"Stop it!" I tapped her on the back of her hand and she immediately let out a howl. Both the mum and the dad turned to look at me. I felt like some kind of criminal.

"I want sweeties!" wailed Sammy.

Urgently, I told Tizz to take her outside. Sammy was dragged off, still wailing. The mum and dad watched her go.

"Doing the shopping all by yourself?" said the mum.

I nodded. I could see her eyes flickering over the contents of our trolley.

"That's a big responsibility," she said.

I drew myself up. "I know how to shop."

"I guess your mum gave you a list?"

I wanted to tell her that I had written my own list, but that might have made her suspicious, so I just said, "Yes," as brightly as I could. "It's my little sister," I added. "She wants things that aren't on there."

The mum laughed. "Tell me about it!"

Fortunately at that point she had to concentrate on packing her bags. I started to take the stuff out of our trolley. Two loaves, two cartons of milk, one pot of marge, half a dozen eggs, two tins of meatballs, cheese triangles, strawberry jam, Cornflakes, fish fingers, and a bottle of squash. It seemed like a lot, but how long would it last? I just hoped Tizz had added it all up correctly, cos how embarrassing would it be if I didn't have enough money? I would die of shame!

But the bill came to *exactly* what Tizz had said it would. I might have known I could rely on her. I don't know where she gets her mathematical brain from. Certainly not from Mum! Mum is as useless at doing sums as I am. We both have to rely on fingers.

I think we were all hoping that Mum would be there, waiting for us, when we got back. I'd even imagined how it would be. I'd pictured her running up the basement steps crying, "Darlings, there you are! I've been so worried about you! Where have you been?"

I even said to Tizz, as we toiled up the road with our heavy bags, that we should have left a note, just in case.

Eagerly, Tizz said, "Why? D'you think she'll have come back?"

I said, "She might have done."

Tizz immediately broke into a run. Sammy cried, "Mum!" and tried to follow but went and tripped over and banged her head, so that by the time I'd put down my bags and kissed her better and picked up the bags and carried on, Tizz was out of sight. I knew as soon as we caught up with her that Mum hadn't come home. Tizz was slumped against the railings at the bottom of the steps.

"Where is she?" said Sammy. "Where's Mum?"

"She's not back yet," I said.

Sammy turned and started pummelling me. "You said she would be! She would be!"

Gently, I corrected her. "I said she *might* be. Let's go in and eat something! We've got all this lovely stuff. Let's decide what we're going to have."

"Choc'lit biscuits!" shouted Sammy.

I guess you can't really expect a five-year-old to be logical. I mean, she *knew* we didn't have any chocolate biscuits. She was just trying it on. Trying to punish me, like I was the one to blame for Mum not being there.

Tizz had gone racing ahead of us into the flat. I caught the tail end of her whizzing into Mum's bedroom. I supposed it *was* just possible Mum had come home and gone straight to bed. Sometimes, when she's been on a high, she can suddenly fall back into a depression, and when she's depressed she can sleep through anything. A herd of elephants wouldn't wake her up.

Tizz came trailing back into the sitting room. "She's not here."

"No! Well." I did my best to make it sound like it was no big deal. "She's only just gone away. It was ten days last time. Could be ten days this time. That's why we've gone and got all this stuff! Keep us going. So when Mum *does* get back she won't feel guilty."

Last time, she'd felt guilty for months afterwards.

We'd gone to visit her in the hospital and she'd rocked to and fro on her chair saying, "How could I leave you? How could I do it to you? I'm a terrible mother! I don't deserve to have children!"

I'd kept begging her to stop blaming herself. I'd told her, over and over, that it wasn't her fault. "You can't help being ill!"

Just cos it's not the sort of illness you can see, like when people have flu or something, doesn't mean it's not real.

"Let's go and get something to eat," I said. "We've got to eat properly! For Mum's sake. Let's d—" I broke off, as Tizz suddenly launched herself across the room. "What are you doing?"

"I want to hear Mum's message again!"

Tizz pressed the button on the phone and Mum's voice filled the room. Light, and bright, almost dizzy with excitement.

"Darlings, darlings! Love you, darlings!"

I couldn't bear to listen. It simply wasn't Mum. That

is, it *was* Mum, but it was Mum teetering on the edge. I felt like any minute she was going to lose her balance and go plunging into a big black hole.

Determinedly, I went through to the kitchen and began unpacking the bags. I prepared what I thought was a really good meal. I mean, considering.

I opened a tin of meatballs, put out a loaf of bread with the marge and the jam, plus three glasses of orange squash. Absolutely *nothing* to complain about. But they were both of them just totally ungrateful.

"Is this all we get?" said Tizz.

"For the moment," I said.

"What's it supposed to be? *Dinner?*"

"Sunday lunch," I said.

"Tastes like *sick*," said Tizz.

"Sick!" Sammy banged her fork down on top of her meatballs and sent one of them flying across the table. I caught it, and put it back on her plate. "Don't want it!" she shrieked. She banged again with her fork. "I want lemonade pie!"

"Sky," snapped Tizz.

I said, "Just shut up, the pair of you, and get on with it!"

Sammy stabbed at a meatball and missed. Tizz said, "You chose this muck! Not me."

She had been so *good* in Tesco! I might have known it wouldn't last. Tizz is one of those people, she has these mood swings. A bit like Mum, I suppose. She doesn't *look* like Mum, apart from the red hair and the freckles. But Mum's hair is golden red; Tizz's hair is more like carrots. And Mum is pretty. Tizz is very small and spiky with little sharp features.

I am just the opposite. Not that I am *large*, but I am not small, either. And not 'specially slim. Just ordinary, really. I don't look a bit like Mum! I wish I did.

Sammy is the only one that looks like her. She doesn't have Mum's red hair – Sammy's hair is coal-black, very sleek and shiny. But she has Mum's blue eyes and heart-shaped face. Quite different from me and Tizz, just like me and Tizz are different from each other. Nobody would ever guess that we are sisters.

I suppose the reason we are different is that we all have different dads. I don't remember my dad cos he left when I was a baby. Just walked out, Mum says. She says that he was never really there in the first place, but he obviously must have been there some of the time or what about me? Where did I come from? When I ask her Mum explains that they were only together for a few short months.

"We were just students. Far too young to have a baby."

Then she hugs me and says, "But I'm very glad we did!"

I do remember Tizz's dad. He was called Andy, and he was small and thin, like Tizz, and had a nasty temper. He wasn't there for very long, either. Tizz feels really bitter that I can remember her dad but she can't, just like we can both remember Sammy's dad but

Sammy can't. Not that it seems to bother Sammy, though it probably will when she is older.

Sammy's dad was OK, I guess. At least he didn't just walk out. He got killed in a fight, which in some ways is even worse. Mum was really upset as she always thought that he was The One. The one that was going to last. Poor Mum! She hasn't had much luck with her boyfriends. I think maybe she hasn't always chosen them very well.

Apart from Cal. Cal was different. He was lovely! We always wished that he could have stayed, but unfortunately he had itchy feet. Least that's what Mum told us. Couldn't bear to be tied down. We missed him horribly after he'd gone.

But Cal was the only one. The rest were all total rubbish. Tizz's dad used to throw things and shout, and Sammy's was too handsome for his own good. That is what Mum's friend Nikki always said. Mum's *so-called* friend. The friend that egged her on to spend money she didn't have. That took her clubbing and didn't even

★ 70 ☆

bother to ring and find out if she'd got home safely. Cos she must have seen that Mum was hyper. She knows Mum has bipolar. She knows what it does to her!

Bipolar is what Mum's illness is called. It's the thing that makes her seesaw up and down. One minute over the moon, the next sunk in depression. I don't *think* Tizz has it, in spite of her mood swings. I think Tizz is the sort of person that is just naturally impatient. It doesn't take much to get her going. Like she'd been OK in Tesco, just for a short while, but then she'd convinced herself that she was going to find Mum waiting for us when we got home and when Mum wasn't there it flipped her back into her normal aggression. Rather like her dad, come to think of it. *Not* like Mum! Mum is never aggressive. She is never impatient, either. Not even when she's super-hyped and is zipping about at a thousand miles per hour while the rest of us are all moving like slugs.

"Hey! Hey!"

I suddenly became aware that Tizz was leaning across the table, poking at me.

"What?" I said. "What?"

"She's not eating anything."

I looked at Sammy. She had taken one bite out of her bread and jam, chewed it to a pulp, and spat it out again on her plate.

"Don't want it," she said.

She was just playing up. Seeing how far she could go. I knew it was frightening for her, Mum disappearing, but I was just so sick of having to make excuses for them both. Her *and* Tizz. It was frightening for all of us!

"If you don't want it," I said, "then don't eat it. Go hungry."

I could see she was a bit thrown by that. She'd obviously thought I was going to plead with her.

"She'll get faint if she doesn't eat," said Tizz.

"So what?" I turned on her, angrily. "What am I supposed to do about it?"

"You're supposed to be looking after her!"

I said, "Why me?"

"Cos you're the oldest," said Tizz. "And this is all your fault! You're the one that's responsible for making sure Mum takes her meds!"

I could have come back at her. I could have said that we were both responsible. But deep inside me there was this nagging voice that said it *was* my fault. I couldn't put all the blame on Nikki. Or Tizz. Suddenly I just felt really tired.

"If she wants something else you'd better go and find something," I said.

"Like what?" said Tizz.

"I don't know! Anything."

Tizz narrowed her eyes. "We can't just eat *anything*," she said. "We've got to make sure there's enough for ten days." She turned, sternly, to Sammy. "If you don't eat what's given to you I'll go and tell Her Upstairs that Mum's not here and then we'll all be taken away and split up!"

I know it isn't good to threaten children but at least it got Sammy to eat. She stuffed her bread and jam into her mouth so fast I hardly saw it leave the plate. Tizz nodded.

"That's better," she said. "Now just drink your orange squash. We don't want any more complaining!"

CHAPTER FIVE

The next day was Monday, and we had to go to school. I set Mum's alarm clock so as to be sure to wake up in time for getting Sammy ready and giving her some breakfast. I was used to doing it cos sometimes when Mum was depressed she wouldn't have the energy to get out of bed and she'd beg me to, "Be a darling and see to Sammy for me." If Tizz was in a good mood she'd help; if she wasn't, she'd just be a nuisance. That morning she was definitely a nuisance.

"I don't think we ought to go to school." She sat up in bed, hugging her knees and giving me this challenging look, like 'Just try making me!'

I said, "Don't be silly, we've got to."

"Why?"

"Why?" Sammy took up the cry, chanting it as she bounced up and down in her bunk. "Why we got to? Why?"

I snapped, "Cos I say so and I'm in charge! Just get up and get dressed."

"Shan't," said Sammy.

"Shan't," said Tizz.

Omigod, she was behaving like a five-year-old. There is some excuse when you *are* five years old. Not when you're ten. When I was ten I was already helping Mum on days when she wasn't up to it. I'd been helping her as long as I could remember. Tizz had *never* taken her fair share of the responsibility.

"GET UP!" I yelled. I really wasn't prepared to stand any nonsense. There are times when you just have to be a bit stern. "Get up, both of you!"

"Shan't."

"Shan't!"

Sammy burrowed back deep into her duvet. Tizz continued with her challenging stare. I wasn't sure what to do. I couldn't *make* them obey me.

"If you don't get up right now..." I said.

"What?" said Tizz.

"What?" shrieked Sammy, from inside her duvet.

"You'll be late," I bawled, "that's what!"

"Can't be late if we're not going," said Tizz.

"Can't be late if we're not going," echoed the thing in its duvet.

Tizz looked at me, smugly. She knew I was at a loss.

"You're not being fair," I said. "You know you wouldn't behave like this if Mum was here."

★ 77 ☆

"Yeah, well, she's not," said Tizz, "is she?"

"Doesn't mean you can just do what you like."

But it seemed that it did. I stood, uncertainly, in the doorway. Now what was I supposed to do? Threatening them obviously wasn't going to get me anywhere. They weren't scared enough of me.

"*Why* don't you want to go?" I said.

Tizz shrugged. "Just don't."

"But why not? You've got to have a reason!"

I thought she was going to go off into a sulk, but Tizz isn't really a sulking sort of person. She's a flaring-up-quickly sort of person. And to be fair, her bad temper never lasts. She muttered something which I didn't catch.

I said, "You what?"

Reluctantly, she muttered it again. "Mum might come back."

"Mum!" Sammy shot out of the duvet like a cork out of a bottle.

"We ought to be here," said Tizz.

I couldn't immediately think what to say to that. It was a huge temptation just to give in and agree that we should all stay home. I didn't want to go to school any more than Tizz or Sammy, cos suppose Mum *did* turn up? She might be confused. She might not realise how long she'd been gone, or what day of the week it was. Then she'd wonder where we were, and she'd get in a panic thinking something had happened. Thinking that we'd been taken away again and she wouldn't be allowed to have us back. And if she'd come down from her high and was feeling depressed, she'd need someone there to look after her.

Tizz could see that I was dithering.

"There's no *point* going to school, we break up next week."

I said, "Yes, I know, but…"

"Not like we're going to miss anything."

"But they'd notice if we don't turn up. They'd try calling Mum."

"What, on her mobile?" said Tizz. "Cos that's the number they've got. And Mum's mobile isn't working!"

She said it triumphantly, like that settled the matter. But I knew I had to be strong. I couldn't let her talk me into it.

"If they kept ringing and she never answered they'd get suspicious. They might send someone to check. Like last term there was this boy in my class that didn't come to school for days? Know what they did? They got the police to go round. The *police!*"

Tizz bit her lip. I could see that I had shaken her, but Tizz is not a person to give in easily.

"So what happened?" she said.

"They found the family wasn't there any more."

"Why?" said Tizz. "Where'd they gone?"

"Dunno, it didn't say. I read it in the paper. But we don't want the police coming round!"

Tizz didn't say anything to this.

"So can we *please* just get dressed?" I said. "I'm going to go and do breakfast."

I did toast and jam and a glass of milk each. It wasn't a lot, but we never had big breakfasts, even when Mum was feeling well. When she was really down we didn't have breakfast at all, unless we got it for ourselves. I was a bit alarmed, though, to see how quickly you could get through a carton of milk. I mean milk is, like, basic. You can't live without milk! I was just glad we had our emergency fund.

I was also glad that both Tizz and Sammy ate their breakfast without any whining. I wasn't in a mood to tolerate whining. I'd had enough of them both and I think they knew it.

"We'll leave a note for Mum," I said. "Just in case."

I printed it out in big letters on the back of an old envelope – DEAR MUM WE HAVE GONE TO SCHOOL WE ARE ALL RIGHT – and propped it up against the radio on the kitchen table where she couldn't miss it.

I said, "First thing she'll see!"

We all left for school together, but Tizz and Sammy

could walk to theirs. I had to catch the bus. I gave Tizz strict instructions to pick Sammy up at the end of the day, and gave Sammy instructions not to tell anyone about Mum.

"Not anyone! OK?"

Sammy put her finger in her mouth and nodded. She seemed a bit uncertain.

"Another thing," I said. "Make sure you eat up all your dinner." We got school dinners for free cos of Mum not working. I didn't want Sammy coming home with her usual tales of 'It was horrible, I couldn't eat it!'

"Promise me," I said.

She nodded again.

"Keep an eye on her," I told Tizz.

Tizz said, "How can I? They have their dinner before we do."

Tizz was in Year six, Sammy was still only Year one. I could see that it was difficult.

"Just do your best," I said. "I don't want to have to worry about you all day."

But I did, of course. I worried about Sammy blurting out to someone that Mum wasn't there. I worried about Tizz forgetting to pick her up, I worried about Sammy wandering off on her own, and most of all I worried about them not being fed properly. How long would our little stock of food last? Had I bought the right stuff? What were we going to do if we ran out?

At lunchtime, as I reached the puddings section, I saw that there were little packets of pink wafer biscuits. The sort that are filled with cream. They were one of Sammy's favourites. I reached out and took one, intending to put it on my tray and save it for Sammy. Instead, at the last minute, I found myself not putting it on the tray but slipping it into my pocket. I looked round, guiltily, wondering if anyone had noticed. I didn't think they had. The only person who might have done was Nina Walters, standing next to me, but Nina wouldn't say anything. Just so long as none of the dinner ladies had seen…

I picked up a pot of strawberry yogurt. I wasn't sure what the rules were about having two lots of puddings. I mean, nobody had ever said, 'Only one pudding per person'. Not as far as I knew. But you could just bet there would be a rule about it, 'specially if you were on free school dinners. They would hate anyone that was getting stuff free going and helping themselves to more than they ought to have. I couldn't stand the shame. Being shown up in front of the whole school! It was bad enough being on free dinners in the first place. People weren't supposed to know, but they always found out.

I almost put the yogurt back, cos I'd really scared myself. It was the first time in my whole life that I had ever stolen anything. But I did want to be able to give Sammy a treat! At the same time, I knew I had to keep my strength up cos who would take care of her and Tizz if I went and faded away through lack of food?

Me and Nina carried our trays to the same table like we usually did. Nina was my friend. Sort of friend.

Well, no, she *was* my friend. Just not a *best* friend. We didn't share secrets or stay over at each other's houses or anything like that. She'd invited me to tea once or twice, but it's difficult when you can't invite someone back. I'd tried that when I was in primary school. I'd brought my best friend Jenny home and it had been just, like, total disaster cos we found Mum in one of her over-the-top moods, tearing about like a hurricane, singing and dancing and laughing in this scary kind of way so that Jenny had got scared and gone running off. She never came round again, and soon after that we'd moved and I stopped trying to be best friends with anyone.

I knew as soon as we sat down that Nina had seen me put the packet of biscuits in my pocket. She wasn't unkind enough to accuse me of it, but when we came to eat our puddings she said, "Yogurt's far more healthy." I could have pretended that I didn't know what she was talking about, but I could feel my face turning bright red.

"They're not for me," I mumbled. "They're for Sammy. It's her birthday on Thursday."

Nina was a really sweet person. She didn't ask me why I'd had to resort to stealing. She just nodded and said, "A birthday treat." I guess she'd worked out that we didn't have much money, like she'd sussed that Mum sometimes wasn't well. But she never poked or pried. She just seemed to accept that if I felt like telling her I would, and if I didn't, I wouldn't, and as far as she was concerned it didn't make any difference. She would have been a great best friend!

I was almost tempted to confide in her, to tell her about Mum and how we'd been left to fend for ourselves. It would have been such a relief to let it all out instead of having to keep it locked away inside me. It was like a big knot of panic tying itself up in my stomach. What if this time Mum *didn't* come back? What if something had happened to her? What if we never saw her again? I couldn't offload all my fears on to Tizz. I knew that for her and Sammy I had to be brave and make like everything was going to be all right. But I did so need someone to speak to!

Nina was giving me this funny look. She said, "Rubes? You OK?"

I nearly told her. I was on the point of it. And then these two girls from our class came and plonked themselves next to us and the moment was gone. It was probably just as well. It would have been different if Nina had been my *best* friend, but I didn't really know how far I could trust her with a secret. Even if I swore her to silence she might still think it was her duty to go home and tell her mum. Not meaning to be disloyal; just cos it would seem the right thing to do. And then the people from the Social Services would come round and take us away and say that Mum wasn't fit to look after us and I just couldn't bear it!

"You sure you're OK?" said Nina, as we went back into class after the lunch break.

I told her that I was but I'm not sure whether she actually believed me. I'm not very good at hiding my feelings. Mum always said she could read me like a book.

Nina put her arm through mine and whispered, "Let me know if there's anything I can do."

She would have been a *really* great best friend.

Last class of the day was P.E. I wondered if I dared bunk off. I was still worried about Sammy, and whether Tizz could be relied on to pick her up. She wasn't used to doing it cos Mum was usually there. I could just imagine Tizz getting caught up with some of her friends and forgetting. And then Sammy would go wandering off and anything could happen.

I decided to take a chance. Miss Crowe, our P.E. teacher, probably wouldn't miss me. I wasn't exactly one of her stars. She was supposed to tick off our names, but she was always so eager to get us all running about that she usually left it till the end of the lesson, by which time I would be safely outside Parkhill Primary waiting for Sammy. Anyway, I didn't care if she did miss me. Sammy was more important than me getting into trouble.

I didn't have long to wait. Sammy and Tizz were two of the first out, Tizz marching ahead with Sammy trailing behind looking tear-stained and sorry for herself. My heart sank. What *now*?

Tizz, scowling, like she suspected I didn't quite trust her, said, "What are you doing here?"

"Got off early," I said. "What's wrong with Sammy?"

"Been sick," said Sammy. She bunched her hands into fists and knuckled at her eyes. "You told me to eat up all my dinner, so I did, and it was slimy pie and veggibles and it made me sick!"

It doesn't honestly take much to make Sammy sick. She has this knack of throwing up whenever she's forced to eat something she doesn't like. She looked at me, triumphantly. "I was sick all over the floor!"

"Never mind," I said. "At least you tried."

"She could have got us into trouble," grumbled Tizz. "They could have called Mum!"

"I was only doing what you said," said Sammy.

I said, "Yes, you were, and look, I've got a treat for

you." I took the packet of pink wafers out of my pocket. Sammy's face immediately lit up.

"Where'd you get those?" said Tizz. "We're not s'pposed to be spending money!"

I told her that I hadn't spent money. "I got them for my lunch."

"So why didn't you eat them?"

"Cos I've been saving them. Here!"

I held them out. Sammy snatched at them, greedily.

"We all ought to have one," said Tizz.

I said, "No, they're for Sammy. To make up for being sick."

Sammy tore open the packet and stuffed a wafer into her mouth. She munched, happily. Tizz and I watched. I could almost see Tizz's mouth watering. Mine was, too!

And then, very nobly, Sammy held out the packet and said, "Share's fair."

I struggled. "That's all right," I said. "You eat them."

Sammy said, "Tizz? You want?"

"Nah!" Tizz slung her school bag over her shoulder. "Let's get back and see if Mum's there."

I felt really proud of them. They were behaving so well!

I might have known it couldn't last. We'd just turned the corner into South Street and were about two minutes away from home when Sammy suddenly went galloping off ahead. I shouted at her to wait for us, cos I had these visions of her catapulting down the basement steps and breaking her neck, the speed she was going. She stopped, briefly, to turn and shout back at me: "I want to see if Mum's come home!" Next thing I knew, she was crashing slap, bang into Her Upstairs.

"That's done it," said Tizz.

We both broke into a run. We were just in time to hear the loud clanging voice of Her Upstairs demanding to know where Mum was. "Is she not home?"

Sammy fell silent.

"She hasn't been there all day." Her Upstairs looked at us, suspiciously. "I've tried several times."

"She's out," said Tizz. "Gone to visit a friend."

"She'll be back later," I said. "Can I give her a message?"

"Yes. You can ask her if she would kindly be sure to put the lid back securely on her bin so we don't have rubbish blowing about all over the place. It's like living in a tip!"

Her Upstairs went stomping off up the steps to the front door. We trailed back down to the basement. In spite of what she'd said about Mum not having been there all day we still went rushing through to the kitchen to see if my note had been moved. It hadn't. It was there, propped against the radio, just as we had left it.

Tizz, in her disappointment, turned angrily on Sammy.

"That was utterly *stupid* of you! *Wanting to see if Mum's come home...*" Tizz put on a Sammy voice, all little girly and lisping. "That's really gone and done it! Thank you *very* much."

"She knew anyway," I said. "She's been battering at the door all day. She knows Mum isn't here."

"Not for certain! For all she knew, Mum could have been asleep and just not heard her. Now she's going to start spying on us. *Honestly!*"

Tizz hurled her bag viciously across the kitchen. Sammy's lip trembled.

"Don't be cross with her," I said. "She couldn't help it."

"She's got to learn! Otherwise she'll get us all locked up."

"Go to prison?" quavered Sammy.

"That's what it feels like… they put you in a home and they won't let you leave!"

I sank down on to the nearest chair. It was all going to pieces. Tizz in a temper, Sammy in tears. Me in despair. I didn't know how much longer I could cope.

CHAPTER SIX

Later that evening, we had temper tantrums. All because
I wanted Sammy to let me wash her hair. When Mum
was feeling good, she made sure we washed our hair
every weekend. When she wasn't feeling good, it was
up to us to remember. Well, up to me mainly. But there
had just been *so much* for me to think about since

Mum had gone. The need to wash Sammy's hair had completely slipped my mind.

It made me feel bad, like I was letting Mum down. She really does like us to be clean and tidy. Unfortunately, last time I'd washed Sammy's hair I'd got soap in her eyes, and now she wouldn't ever let me forget it.

"You're rough, go away, I don't want my hair washed!"

"But it needs it," I said. "I won't get soap in your eyes again, I promise!"

"What's happening?" said Tizz, appearing at the door.

I told her that Sammy was refusing to let me wash her hair.

"I washed mine," said Tizz.

She made it sound like she deserved a gold star. "Look at you," she said. "You're a right mess!

"So are you!" yelled Sammy.

"At least I'm clean! You're disgusting!"

I said, "Please, Sammy. *Please* let me wash your hair."

"Shan't!"

Before we could stop her, she'd gone racing out of

the bedroom and into the loo. Tizz at once charged after her and hammered on the door.

"Samantha Tindall, you come out of there!"

Sammy shrieked, "Go away!"

Tizz looked at me like, now what do we do? It's not very often Tizz is at a loss. I shook my head; we could hardly break the door down.

"I guess we just have to leave her," I said. "Let's go and watch telly."

"She can't be allowed to get away with it," protested Tizz. "She has to do what she's told!"

"Tell her," I said.

Tizz banged again on the door. "You wouldn't behave like this if Mum was here!"

"That's why she's doing it," I said.

"Just taking advantage!" Tizz rattled the door handle, in a fury. "Just playing up!"

"It's not her fault," I said. "She doesn't understand what's going on. She wants Mum. She's scared!"

"You think she's the only one?"

Tizz rounded on me, and I saw that tears had sprung into her eyes. That shook me. Tizz never cries. She's never scared!

"Mum will come back," I said. "She came back before, she'll come back this time."

"How do you know?" muttered Tizz.

I didn't. But I had to believe it!

"Sammy." I tried the door handle, very gently. "Sammy, please come out! No one's cross with you. And you don't have to have your hair washed tonight if you don't want to. We can do it tomorrow. Please, Sammy?"

In muffled tones she said, "Go 'way! I'm doing things."

She emerged a few seconds later to announce, defiantly, that there wasn't any toilet paper left.

"I used it all up."

"Did you wash your hands?" said Tizz.

"Yes, I did, and you're a rude girl asking me!"

"I'm just trying," said Tizz, "to look *after* you. And now we haven't any toilet paper! What are we supposed to do without toilet paper?"

"Don't worry," I said. "I'll get some."

"But what are we going to do till then?"

I told her there was a box of tissues by Mum's bed. "We can use those."

But the tissues stayed where they were, on Mum's bedside table. Neither me nor Tizz wanted to go into Mum's room and see her bed, all rumpled from when she'd last slept in it. I promised that I would bring some toilet paper home with me tomorrow.

"More expense," grumbled Tizz.

"I didn't say I was going to *buy* it," I said. "I said I'd bring some home with me."

We didn't have the money to waste on luxuries like toilet paper. Or toothpaste. Or washing-up liquid. We were running out of everything! Next morning, soon as I got to school I went down to the girls' cloakroom in the basement and shut myself in one of the cubicles. Hooray! There was an almost full toilet roll. I didn't take the actual roll cos that would have been too bulky, but I tore off most of it and sat there folding it neatly and stuffing it down the side of my bag. It felt like a kind of weird thing to be doing, and I know that toilet roll isn't an *absolute* necessity, like food and drink, but I just couldn't see how we were to manage without it.

I'd been bracing myself to be called into the Office cos of bunking off early the previous day, but nobody said anything so it seemed like I'd got away with it. I asked Nina at breaktime.

"Didn't Miss Crowe want to know where I was?"

"Don't think she missed you," said Nina.

"What about when she did the register?"

Nina giggled. "I put on your voice and answered for you!"

"You pretended to be me?" I was like, gobsmacked. It's true that Miss Crowe is a bit daffy, but even so, if she'd noticed I wasn't there Nina could have got into real trouble.

"You didn't have to do that," I said.

Nina shrugged. "No problem."

I promised that I would do the same for her one

day, but she just said, "Whatever." She didn't even ask me where I'd gone or why I'd bunked off. I told her anyway, cos it seemed only fair.

"I had to go and pick Sammy up. Mum couldn't get there and I was worried Tizz might forget and go off without her."

Nina nodded. "I thought it was probably something like that." She linked her arm through mine. "How is your mum? Is she all right?"

I said, "Yes, she's fine." And then, before I could stop myself, "It's just she has some days when she's not so good as other days. That's all."

"And then you have to take care of Sammy."

"Well… you know! Just occasionally. But I'm quite used to it," I said. "It doesn't bother me."

"I think you must be a very good sister," said Nina.

I was embarrassed by that. Quickly I said, "I'm sure you would be, too!"

"D'you reckon?"

I said, "I'm sure you would!"

"'Cept I'm an only child. D'you think being an only child makes you selfish?"

I squeezed her arm. "Not in your case!"

Later on, standing with Nina in the lunch queue, I stole a sandwich. I didn't mean to. It wasn't something I'd planned. It just happened. My hand seemed to reach out all by itself, without me having any control over it. I saw my fingers close over the sandwich box, like one of those grabbing machines you get at the end of piers. The ones that scrabble about amongst all the prizes at the bottom of the cage and there's just this one thing you're desperate for it to pick up and it absolutely never does. Even if it did, you could be sure it would drop it before it was hauled to safety.

I didn't drop my sandwich. My fingers closed over it good and hard and whizzed it quick as a flash into my bag. Nobody saw; not even Nina. I thought how horrified Mum would be if she knew that I had turned into a thief. I felt that I ought to be ashamed, but all I could think was, suppose we ran out of food? I was responsible for Tizz and Sammy. I couldn't let them starve!

Me and Nina sat together, as usual. We had the last seats at the end of a table full of Year eights, so it was like we were on our own. Thinking about it, me and Nina mostly were. I'm not sure why. Maybe it was because all the others reckoned we were a bit odd. Back when I was in primary school someone had started a rumour that my mum was mad, which is the kind of thing that follows you around. As for Nina, she'd been home-educated for most of her life and hadn't been sure, to begin with, how you were supposed to behave in a class of thirty other kids. I guess it was only natural we stuck together. I was really glad we had, cos I don't know what I'd have done without her during those first terrible days when Mum wasn't there.

Halfway through lunch Nina dug me in the ribs and said, "Hey, Ruby, want my pudding?"

She pushed it towards me. A tiny little sponge cake with pink icing. I'd thought at the time it was a strange choice, cos Nina was like, really health conscious. It was something to do with being educated at home and always being given fruit and nuts and stuff.

"Don't you want it?" I said.

"I do," said Nina, "but I mustn't. I'm getting a spare tyre. Feel!"

I felt. "There isn't anything there!"

"That's what you think. If I carry on like this I won't be able to do my skirt up."

"That is such rubbish," I said. "You don't eat hardly enough to feed a flea."

"Excuse me," said Nina, "I pigged out on a whole Mars Bar last night."

I just didn't believe it. Her mum would never let her.

"I did," said Nina. "I had a binge. Oh, please, Rubes, do take it! You could keep it for Sammy, for her birthday. You could buy some little candles for it."

It was true; I could. I was really tempted.

"It'll go to waste," said Nina. "Unless *you* want to eat it?"

"No! I'll take it for Sammy."

"Have you got something you can wrap it in?"

I opened my bag and pulled out a wodge of toilet paper. Nina's eyes widened. I didn't know for sure whether she'd seen the sandwich, but she could hardly help noticing the toilet paper.

My brain clicked into furious overdrive. How was I supposed to explain that? I giggled, trying to turn it into a joke.

"I haven't got the squitters, if that's what you're thinking! I had to buy a toilet roll on my way into school, cos we've, like, run out? But then it wouldn't go into my bag so I had to unravel it all and kind of squash it down, kind of thing."

Nina said, "Good thinking! Just make sure you don't squash Sammy's cake. Honestly, I shouldn't ever have taken it! I am just so *weak*. In future, I'm going to stick to fruit. You're supposed to eat *five helpings*." Her eyes widened. "*Five. Every day.* And all I do is pig out on Mars Bars!"

I knew she didn't, really. She was just saying it to make me feel better. Not that it did, cos I knew what she was doing. Also, I was suddenly starting to feel bad about the stuff I was giving to Tizz and Sammy. When we'd gone shopping on Sunday we hadn't even considered fruit or vegetables. I needed to get some, right away!

Nina was looking at me. She seemed concerned. "Did I say something wrong?"

"No." I shook my head. "You just reminded me that I was supposed to get fruit and vegetables as well as toilet roll, and I stupidly didn't bring enough money with me!"

I'd hidden our emergency fund, all £5 of it, in a pair of socks under my mattress. I would have to go home and get it and then go out again, cos we really needed those fresh fruit and vegetables! Mum would be so upset if she thought we hadn't been eating properly.

Even at times when we were desperately broke she'd always done her best to make sure we had *some* healthy food to eat.

"I could lend you something," said Nina. "How much d'you want? I've got... £2! Would that be enough?"

I accepted it, gratefully. "I'll pay you back tomorrow, I promise!"

"That's all right," said Nina.

"No, I will," I said. "Honestly!"

"Tell you what," said Nina, "you ought to go down the market. It's really cheap down there, 'specially at the end of the day. That's what my mum says. She says they like to get rid of stuff before it goes rotten. Bush Street Market? Have you ever been there?"

I shook my head. I'd never even heard of it.

"I could show you, if you like," said Nina. "It's on my way home."

Nina lived in totally the opposite direction from us. I was a bit concerned that it would make me late back, but I really did want to get some healthy food.

We couldn't live out of tins all the time. Mum would be horrified. She always said that tins were for standby.

"See? Look!" Nina waved a hand as we got off the bus and went down some steps to the market. "Loads of stuff!"

We walked up and down, searching for anything that was going cheap. Nina found some carrots, and I found some apples and bananas.

"Oh, and tomatoes!" Nina grabbed me by the hand and dragged me across to one of the stalls. "How much have we got left?"

I counted it out. "40p." I loved the way she'd said we, like we were in this together. It made me feel less on my own. But the tomatoes were way more than we could afford. I stared at them, wistfully. They were so lovely and red, and all plump and juicy!

"'Scuse me." Nina marched up boldly, and held out the 40p. "How many tomatoes could we get for this?"

The man on the stall looked like he might enjoy biting the heads off chickens. Like really scary! I got all tense, expecting him to tell us to push off, but after studying us for a bit he said, "How many d'you want?"

"Many as we can get, please," said Nina.

It came as a shock, Nina being so daring. At school she was quiet as a mouse. But it worked! We went away with a big bag of lovely ripe tomatoes. Nina said, "There! Now you can have tomato salad and tomato sandwiches and tomatoes every single day till you get sick of them! D'you want to come back to my place for tea?"

I hadn't expected that. I hesitated.

"Might as well," said Nina. "Now you're here."

It was a great temptation, but I thought probably I ought to get back before Tizz and Sammy started wondering where I was. Nina came with me to the bus stop and waited till a bus came that was going in the right direction. She called after me, "Don't squash the tomatoes... or Sammy's cake!"

I couldn't wait to get home. I was so proud of myself! I had apples, I had carrots, I had bananas and I had tomatoes. What could be healthier?

As I clattered down the basement steps I felt a sudden surge of hope. Maybe today would be the day when Mum had come back! She would have been there, waiting, when Tizz and Sammy got home from school. Now they would all be sitting at the kitchen table, Mum drinking a cup of her peppermint tea that she loved, Tizz and Sammy telling her how I'd looked after them. Cos I *had* looked after them! I'd done my very best. They would just be starting to grow impatient. Mum would be saying, "Where's Ruby? Why isn't she home yet?" Then Tizz, with her sharp ears, would hear my footsteps and come rushing to let me in. And there would be Mum, running to meet me, holding out her arms, a big beam on her face.

"Ruby, darling, I'm back!"

But she wasn't. Instead, I found Sammy in tears

and Tizz in a fury, with her face all pinched and scrunched.

"*Where have you been?*" She snarled it at me. I shut the door, quickly, in case Her Upstairs might be lurking.

"I've been to the market! I got us some fruit and veg. Look, see, tomatoes!" I waved the bag at her. Tizz punched at it, angrily.

"It's nearly five o'clock!"

"I couldn't help it, I had to get two buses." And now she'd gone and scattered my precious tomatoes all over the floor. Some of them had actually burst. "Why is Sammy crying?" I said. "What have you done to her?

"*Me?*" Tizz screamed it at the top of her voice. "I haven't done anything! You're the one that's upset her. She thought you weren't coming back!"

"Oh, Sammy—" I put down my bag and folded her into my arms. "I'm sorry, I'm so sorry!"

"She thought you'd run away," said Tizz.

"No!" I was horrified. It had never occurred to me

that Sammy might think that. "I'd never run away from you! Not ever!"

But how was she to know? Mum disappearing had turned her whole little world upside down. She probably felt she couldn't trust anyone any more. Either me or Tizz, or even both of us, could suddenly walk out and not come back.

I cooked her fish fingers for tea; the whole packet. It seemed the least I could do. And I didn't nag her to eat any fruit. Me and Tizz shared my stolen sandwich and ate a banana each. The bananas were a bit black and mushy, so I said maybe we'd better finish them off before they went rotten, but Tizz said, "No, thank *you*," and opened a tin of sausages without asking my permission.

I could have said something. I could have told her she was being greedy and selfish, but just for the moment all the fight had gone out of me. I ate the bananas myself. They were rather horrible, but there are worse things in life. Maggots, for instance. If you were really starving you would eat maggots. Black bananas were almost a delicacy in comparison. At least, that is what I told myself.

That night, Sammy crept into my bed and fell asleep curled up against me. It wasn't really comfortable, but I didn't have the heart to turn her out. I was just glad she didn't hate me any more.

CHAPTER SEVEN

On Thursday it was going to be Sammy's birthday. Thursday was tomorrow, and we hadn't got a single present for her! Just the little pink cake that Nina had given me, which I'd carefully wrapped in tinfoil and hidden at the back of the kitchen cupboard.

But the little pink cake would only last about two mouthfuls. She had to have more than that! I decided that at lunch time I would see if I could find something else as an extra treat for her birthday tea. I wouldn't steal it; I'd finished with stealing. I would take an apple and some carrots into school with me, and I would eat those and bring my lunch back home for Sammy. Nobody could object to that.

In the meantime, treats were all very well but you couldn't expect a six-year-old to have a birthday without any presents. That would be terrible.

"We've got to get something for her," I said.

"With what?" said Tizz. "You went and spent all our emergency fund on rotting veg!"

It was true that the bananas hadn't been very pleasant, and the tomatoes, my beautiful ruby red tomatoes, were already turning suspiciously soft and squishy. Even the carrots had brown patches. But I did think it was mean of Tizz to draw attention to it.

"I didn't spend *all* the emergency fund," I said. Even

after I'd paid Nina back, we'd still have £3 left. But we really needed to keep that cos it would be horribly scary not to have anything at all. "You don't think Mum might have got her something before—" I waved a hand. I didn't like to say it out loud. *Before Mum had disappeared.*

"Might have done," said Tizz.

"Maybe we should go and look?"

"You go," said Tizz.

"No, both of us!" I said.

I knew Tizz didn't want to, but I didn't, either. I told her she was being unfair.

"I'm doing my best! I can't do everything."

"Oh, all *right*," said Tizz.

Together, we crept into Mum's room. Even though I knew Mum couldn't possibly have come back during the night without our knowing, there was still a bit of me that hoped against hope we might find her there, curled up beneath the duvet, peacefully asleep. I saw the way Tizz let her eyes flicker towards the bed, and guessed she'd been hoping the same thing. I reached out for her hand and squeezed it.

"She will come back," I said. "She will!"

Tizz said, "Yeah, yeah. Let's get this over with."

She grabbed the stool from Mum's dressing table and dragged it across to the wardrobe. It was an old wardrobe, very big and heavy. On the top, safely out of reach, was where Mum used to keep our Christmas and birthday presents. She really thought we didn't know!

I watched anxiously as Tizz stood on tiptoe on the stool and peered over the top of the wardrobe.

"Is there anything there?"

"Nope." She jumped back down. "Nothing."

"What are we going to do?" I heard my voice, pitifully wailing. Sammy couldn't have a birthday without any presents!

"Dunno." Tizz banged the stool back into place. "Don't see there's anything much we can do."

"You don't think, when you have lunch…"

"What?"

"You could, like… take something for Sammy? Something nice, like a – a KitKat, or something?"

"Don't have KitKats," said Tizz.

"Well, whatever! A pudding or something."

Tizz looked at me like I'd gone mad.

"If we can't give her presents," I pleaded, "we ought at least to give her a birthday tea!"

Tizz said she would think about it. As we left the room we bumped into Sammy, on her way out of the bathroom. Her hair was dripping wet.

"I washed it myself," she said.

"Oh Sammy," I said, "good girl!"

"Not before time," said Tizz. "You were starting to look like a bird's nest. Goodness only knows what you had growing in there!"

"Go 'way," said Sammy. "You're rude! And why were you in Mum's room?" She stared up at me, trustfully. "Has Mum come back?"

"Not yet," I said. "But she will!"

Next day, I took Nina's money into school with me. I had to press it on her. She really didn't want to accept it.

"Honestly," she said, "you don't have to pay me back right away."

But I felt that I had to. In spite of sometimes running out of things, like milk and eggs and stuff, and having to throw herself on the mercy of Her Upstairs, Mum had this strict rule about never borrowing money.

"Get yourself into deep trouble if you start doing that!"

So I forced Nina to take her £2, only to immediately wish that I hadn't. If I'd kept it I could have bought something for Sammy!

In CDT that morning I pinched a sheet of card and at breaktime I cut it and folded it and wrote, *HAPPY BIRTHDAY SIX YEARS OLD!* in red felt tip on the front. Inside, I put *Hugs & kisses and loads of love from Ruby xxx.*

"Is that for Sammy?" said Nina.

I nodded. "I forgot to buy her a proper one."

"Home-made's much better," said Nina. "You just need to put a bit of decoration on it, like…" She took some different coloured pens out of her bag. "Can I do it?"

Nina is so good at drawing! She made a border of butterflies and little birds. I said, "That looks really professional! Sammy will love it."

At lunchtime I took a cheese sandwich and a pot of Strawberry Frootie. The sandwich was in a plastic box, so I reckoned it would keep all right for just one day. I thought that I would get another one tomorrow and then we could all share them and have a proper birthday tea together, the three of us. It would be nicer for Sammy than me and Tizz just sitting there watching her. We could pretend it was a little party, and put candles on her cake and sing Happy Birthday. Sammy would enjoy that.

I felt quite proud and happy. I could cope! I was 'specially pleased about the cheese sandwich, cos cheese is healthy. It's also one of the few things Sammy will eat without complaining. And Strawberry Frooties are all sweet and pink and yucky, so I knew she would enjoy that. Anything sweet, and especially pink!

I could hardly expect Nina not to notice when I put the sandwich and the Frootie in my bag. I explained that I'd brought the carrots and apples with me cos I wasn't sure how much longer they would last.

"I reckoned I ought to eat them up first. I can always eat the sandwich later."

Nina agreed that that was probably a good idea. "D'you want a mouthful of curry?"

"Not sure I'll have room," I said, "with all these carrots."

Omigod, those carrots were disgusting! Not only did they have brown bits in them, they'd gone all soft and bendy. It was like chewing rubber.

"Just a mouthful," urged Nina.

In the end I had several mouthfuls. I couldn't

resist! I absolutely adore curry, it had been a great struggle not to grab one when I was in the lunch queue.

"Phew!" Nina pushed her plate towards me. "Finish it off, *please*. I'm positively bloated!"

She was *such* a bad liar. But the curry was bliss, especially after three days of nothing but toast and marge and rotting fruit. I was beginning to understand how difficult it must be for Mum, trying to feed us all a healthy diet on so little money. We'd always been broke, as long as I could remember. Even when Tizz's horrible dad had been around. Even when Mum was working. It was always a struggle. But I couldn't remember that we'd ever gone hungry.

As usual, on my way home after school my heart started thudding, boompboompboomp, and a prickle of sweat broke out all over me. Would *today* be the day Mum came back? The blood pounded in my ears as I hurtled down the basement steps. Tizz flung open the door before I'd even got my key out.

"We're *starving*," she said. "What are we going to have for tea?"

Crossly I said, "Why ask me?" Yesterday she'd just helped herself. A whole tin of sausages! I chucked my bag into a corner, before remembering, too late, that I had a Strawberry Frootie in there. I rushed across to rescue it.

"I thought you were supposed to be in charge?" said Tizz.

"Doesn't seem to make much difference," I said. "Nobody takes any notice."

"Oh. Well! In that case—" Tizz tossed her head. "We'll eat what we like."

I said, "Where's Sammy?"

"Watching telly."

"Good."

I took out the Frootie and the cheese sandwich.

"What are those for?" said Tizz.

"They're for Sammy. For her birthday tea. Did you get her anything?"

"No, I couldn't. People were watching."

I said, "Huh!" as I hid the Frootie and the sandwich on the top shelf of the kitchen cupboard, where Sammy couldn't see them. "For your information," I said, "they were watching me, too."

"Big deal," said Tizz.

Whatever that was supposed to mean. She was just miffed cos I'd got something for Sammy and she hadn't.

"I've made her a card, as well," I said. "See?"

"From both of us?" said Tizz.

"No. Just me."

I guess it was a bit mean, but then Tizz had been even meaner, not getting anything for Sammy's birthday.

We ate tea in glum silence. I boiled three eggs and one of them burst. Normally I'd have had the burst one, but today I didn't offer. I said we'd toss for it. Just me and Tizz, and I won. But it seemed I hadn't boiled them long enough. Sammy wouldn't eat hers cos she complained it was runny.

"And there's something nasty in it!"

"It's only a speck of blood," said Tizz.

"*Blood?*" Sammy shrieked and shoved the egg away so violently it spilled across the table. I had to open some pilchards for her. Our one and only tin! Tizz calmly spooned up the spilt egg and then, without asking, helped herself to a cheese triangle. I ate tomatoes. I think some of them must have been going putrid cos they tasted really disgusting, but we couldn't afford to just chuck them out. The food situation was really starting to get serious. It was frightening how a cupboard that had been quite full on Sunday could suddenly look half empty only three days later. It wasn't even like we'd been pigging out. I wasn't surprised when Tizz announced that she was still hungry.

"I can feel the sides of my stomach flapping!"

Sammy said that the sides of her stomach were flapping, too.

"What have we got?" Tizz marched across to the cupboard. "*Cornflakes. Soup. Baked beans.* Yuck, yuck, double yuck! There's nothing here worth eating."

I told her she could have an apple. "I'll cut one up and we'll all share it."

"Oh, *big deal*," said Tizz.

I did wish she would stop saying that. I didn't know what it meant, but it sounded really sarcastic.

The apple was OK; sort of. I glared at Tizz, daring her to say anything, but she just chewed, in silence. Sammy whined that it was sour, which I have to admit it was, so we tried dipping it in jam.

"There," I said. "That's quite nice, isn't it?"

Sammy nodded, doubtfully. Tizz, meanwhile, had pushed back her chair and was heading for the door.

"Where are you going?" I said.

"Out," said Tizz.

"Out where?"

"Just out. I won't be long."

I couldn't really stop her. I left Sammy sitting on the sofa watching television and went into the bedroom. I'd decided that if I couldn't afford to *buy* her a present I would have to give her something that

★ 125 ☆

belonged to me. Something that I knew she liked, such as...

My fan! My Spanish fan! I took it out and flicked it open. It was made of paper and was quite fragile, which was why I never let Sammy play with it even though she was always begging me. She'd been after that fan for simply ages.

I sank down on to my bed, wondering if I could bear to part with it. It had been a present from Cal; he'd brought it back from Spain with him. I loved it for its own sake, but I loved it even more cos of it being Cal that had given it to me.

Cal really, truly *was* the best boyfriend Mum had ever had. THE BEST. I had known Cal ever since I could remember. He'd been around before Sammy was born. He didn't actually live with us in those days, though me and Tizz would have liked him to. But he was just always there. And then Mum had taken up with Sammy's dad, the one me and Tizz referred to as the Hunk, and for a while we didn't see Cal any more. Mum said he'd gone off on his travels.

The Hunk was OK, I suppose, and we didn't actually mind him, except that he wasn't Cal; but he drank too much and was always getting into fights, so really it wasn't surprising that he came to a sad end, though that didn't stop it being upsetting for Mum.

It was after the Hunk had gone that Cal came back into our lives. He actually moved in for a bit, just for a few short months. He took care of Mum, and he took care of me and Tizz and Sammy. It was like having a proper dad for the first time. Me and Tizz had really hoped that he was there to stay. We even had this dream of him and Mum getting married, so that we could all settle down and be like a real family. But for some reason things didn't work out. Mum said that Cal wasn't really a settling-down kind of person. It was because of him having these itchy feet, which kept making him want to get up and go.

"Can't manage to stay in one place for more than five minutes."

Cal's fan was one of my most treasured possessions. I knew if I gave it to Sammy it would only get broken. But what else did I have? She'd always fancied my music box that played *Rudolph the Red-Nosed Reindeer*, but last time I'd tried playing it there'd been a lot of hiccupping and wheezing so it was obviously going wrong. And my glass ball with the snowstorm inside it was scratched, and the little china donkey with the straw hat had a chip out of one of his ears, and really just about everything I owned seemed to be broken, or battered, or not properly working. All I had was my Spanish fan.

I heaved a big trembly sigh. I wanted Sammy to be happy, but I desperately didn't want to part with my fan! On the other hand, I couldn't bear the thought of her little face, all innocent and beaming, expecting presents, and there not being any. It seemed I didn't really have any choice. It was the fan or nothing.

I checked that Sammy was still safely in front of the

television and went through to the kitchen. While I was wrapping her present, Tizz appeared.

"Where have you been?" I said.

"Just up the road."

"What for?"

"What's it to you?" said Tizz. "I s'ppose I can go up the road if I want?"

"If I was going up the road," I said, "I'd tell you what I was going there for."

"Why?" Tizz said aggressively.

"Cos I wouldn't want you to be worried," I said.

"Like you didn't want us to be worried when you got home later, buying all those rotten vegetables and spending all our money and we didn't even know where you were."

I felt my cheeks burst into flame. How mean she was! Keeping on about my vegetables.

"That was a sudden decision," I mumbled.

"Yeah. Same here," said Tizz. Her eyes narrowed. "Where'd you get that wrapping paper? Did you buy it?"

I said, "No, I did not! It's what was left over at Christmas."

"I want some!"

Tizz made a snatch at it. I whisked it out of her reach.

"What d'you want it for?"

"Got something for Sammy."

"What?"

"Nothing to do with you. Gimme some wrapping paper!"

"Not until you tell me what you've got."

Slyly, testing my reaction, Tizz put her hand in her pocket and pulled out a big butterfly hair slide. I looked at her, horrified.

"Where did that come from?"

Tizz stamped a foot. "Stop interrogating me!"

I was so surprised she knew such a word that just for a moment it threw me.

"Going on at me all the time. Anyone'd think I was a criminal!"

"But you didn't have any money," I said

"That's what you think," said Tizz.

"Are you saying you had some you didn't tell us about?"

"Might be."

I didn't believe her. "You stole it," I said, "didn't you?"

"Did not!"

I felt sure that she had. But what could I say? I'd stolen pink wafers. *And* a sandwich.

Without Mum, this whole family was going to pieces.

"Are you going to me give some of that paper?" said Tizz.

I let her have it. There didn't seem any reason not to. I was every bit as bad as she was.

"*Thank* you," said Tizz. "Now I can wrap my present. I got a card, as well." She waved it at me. "A proper one!"

"Maybe tomorrow," I said, "you'll get a KitKat."

"Yeah." Tizz nodded. "I might just do that."

CHAPTER EIGHT

Next morning was Sammy's birthday, so we gave her her presents before we went to school. She insisted on wearing her butterfly hair clip straightaway, and begged me to let her take my fan – *her* fan – with her to show her friends. I hadn't the heart to say no, though

I couldn't help wondering whether she would bring it back in one piece.

"When you get home," I promised her, "we've got a special birthday tea for you."

"Will Mum be here?" said Sammy.

"Well… she might," I said. "But you mustn't be disappointed if she isn't. Wherever she is, I'm sure she'll be thinking of you."

"She might even ring," said Tizz. "We might get back and find a birthday message."

Oh, I did wish she hadn't said that! Sammy's face immediately lit up. She raced across to the phone.

"Make sure the machine's switched on!"

"It's on," I said. "We'll check for messages when we get back."

We did, but of course there weren't any. I hadn't really expected there to be.

"She probably hasn't been able to recharge her

phone," I said. "Did you remember to bring your fan home?"

"Got it in my bag," said Sammy.

"Shall we put it somewhere safe?"

"No!" She snatched up her bag and held it very tightly. I knew then, for sure, that she'd had an accident. But it was her birthday, so I wasn't going to embarrass her. I gave her a little push.

"Go and watch some telly while we get your tea."

The tea, when we set it out on the table, didn't look anywhere near as impressive as I'd hoped. We had:

1 cheese sandwich

1 egg and cress sandwich (brought back by me that same day)

1 Strawberry Frootie

1 Strawberry yogurt (also brought back by me)

1 small pink cake

1 bar of KitKat (supplied by Tizz)

1 packet of crisps (also supplied by Tizz)

I didn't ask Tizz where she'd got the KitKat and the crisps; it seemed safer not to know. I used the last of the orange squash and stuck six matchsticks into the pink cake. I hadn't been able to find any candles, but I thought perhaps matchsticks would do just as well.

We let Sammy eat as much as she wanted, which was practically everything. Me and Tizz shared the egg and cress sandwich and the yogurt and one finger of KitKat. Sammy kept saying "Share's fair!" and pushing stuff at us, but even Tizz nobly waved it away.

"You're the birthday girl," she said.

After we'd sung Happy Birthday and Sammy had blown out the matchsticks and given me and Tizz a tiny nibble of cake each, we watched some of her favourite DVDs including an especially yucky one about a family of squirrels. A daddy squirrel, a mummy squirrel, and a tiny little baby squirrel called Sam. It made me and Tizz want to throw up, but Sammy loved it to bits. She kept squealing happily and clapping her hands every time anyone said her name.

"*Sam!*"

"Yeah, but it's a boy," said Tizz.

She just had to, didn't she? Just couldn't resist. Sammy went all quiet after that. She sat on the sofa, cuddled up next to me, sucking her thumb. She'd been doing a lot of thumb sucking, just lately. It was like she'd gone back to babyhood. But I didn't try and stop her; it would have seemed unkind.

When we went to bed – I'd given up the battle of trying to make her go at her usual time – she refused to get into her bunk and clambered in again with me.

It was a horrible night. I was so hungry I found it difficult to sleep. I had to keep resisting the urge to go and raid the cupboard. We didn't have much left in there, and I really *really* didn't want to start stealing again. It not only made me feel bad, it frightened me that I might get caught.

I woke up next morning with a feeling of deep despair. It was like I'd pinned everything on to Sammy's birthday. Giving her a good time, making her happy.

That had been my one aim. Now that it was over, there didn't seem to be anything left. I couldn't go on fighting!

I wondered if that was how Mum felt when she fell into one of her depressions. Suddenly I could understand how she just wanted to curl up in bed and sleep. I so didn't want to have to get up and go to school.

And then I turned over and felt my nightie clinging to me, all cold and clammy. I peeled back the duvet and sure enough, there was a damp patch. Wetting the bed was something Sammy hadn't done since she was tiny.

I got her up and dried her off, hoping Tizz wouldn't notice and make one of her tactless remarks, but of course she demanded to know why I was stripping my bed.

"Time it got changed," I said.

"What about mine?" said Tizz. "Why aren't you changing mine?"

"If you want it changed, do it yourself!" I snapped.

I wasn't in any mood to put up with her and her selfishness.

I staggered off to the washing machine only to discover that we were out of washing powder. We were almost out of washing-up liquid, too. We were almost out of everything. It was scary. I squeezed in what little washing-up liquid there was just as Tizz appeared, sullenly dragging her sheet.

"You might have brought Sammy's," I said.

Tizz said, "Why?"

"Cos hers needs changing just as much as ours!"

Tizz turned and yelled. "*SAMMY*! Bring your sheet! Don't see why I should be expected to do everything," she said.

The nerve of it! Like she'd done *anything*.

Crossly, I stuffed all three sheets into the machine and slammed the door. When I turned round I found Tizz with a felt tip pen crossing days off on the calendar. She'd marked the following Tuesday with a big red X.

"What's that for?" I said.

"That's when Mum's due back." Tizz looked at me, challengingly. "*Ten days*. Right?"

It was like she was daring me to contradict her.

I said, "Oh. Right."

I wanted to believe it every bit as much as she did. Tuesday was the day when Mum would come back. I reckoned we could just about hold out until then. I wasn't sure that we'd be able to go on very much longer. If Mum wasn't back by Tuesday, we'd be forced to give in and tell someone. Probably Her Upstairs. And that would be the end of everything.

At school Nina wanted to know how the birthday tea had gone.

"Did Sammy have a good time? Did you put candles on her cake?"

I said, "No, we put matchsticks," and Nina giggled, thinking I was being funny. And then she realised that I wasn't, and she stopped giggling and looked embarrassed, and I wished I hadn't said it. What did I have to go and tell Nina about the matchsticks for? Now I'd made her feel uncomfortable.

We didn't talk about Sammy's birthday any more after that. Instead we talked about how it was going to be the end of term next week, and I asked Nina if she was going away, cos I knew it was what people did in the summer holidays, but that just made her feel even more uncomfortable. She knew I wouldn't be going anywhere.

"I expect we might go somewhere," she said. "Maybe. I don't really know."

But of course she did. Nina always went away. Last summer she'd gone to Spain for a month. And at Christmas she'd gone skiing. She'd sent me a postcard with a foreign stamp.

"I suppose we might go camping," she said. "That's what we sometimes do. Wouldn't it be fun if you could come with us?"

I said that it would, but at that point two other girls from our class came and sat next to us and started talking, and I was quite relieved. I knew there wasn't any chance I could ever go off camping with Nina. I thought she probably knew it, too.

When I got home that afternoon I bumped into Her Upstairs angrily stomping up the basement steps.

"Is your mother deliberately avoiding me?" she said.

I said, "No! Of course not."

"So where is she, then? Why is she never at home?"

"She's very busy," I said. "She's got this friend that's in hospital. She has to keep visiting her."

"Oh, really? Well, that's odd! According to your sister — who, incidentally, has a bit of a mouth on her — she's out looking for jobs."

"Yes," I said, "that as well. She's visiting her friend in hospital *and* looking for jobs. That's why she's not here."

Her Upstairs made a noise like "Hrrmf!" Like she didn't believe me. "And what's happened to that girl's face?" she said. She paused, at the top of the steps, and looked down at me. "Has someone been knocking her about?"

"She prob'ly fell over," I said. "She's always falling over."

With that, I scuttled on down the steps as fast as I could and banged at the door. It opened just a crack.

"Oh, it's you," said Tizz. "I thought it was her come back."

I took one look at her and shrieked, "Omigod, what have you done?" One side of her face was all scratched and torn, like a wild cat had landed on her. "What happened?"

"Had a fight," said Tizz.

My heart plummeted. That was all we needed! Tizz getting into a fight.

"Wasn't my fault," muttered Tizz.

I just bet it was! I said, "So whose fault was it?"

"This girl. Alanna Gibbs."

"Why? What did she do?"

"She said Mum was a benefit scrounge."

I said, "A *what*?"

"A benefit scrounge! She said people like her mum

that worked really hard have to pay for people like our mum to sit at home and do nothing. Just live on benefits."

That really took me aback. I said, "She never!"

"She so did."

"And you went for her?"

"Well, wouldn't you?" said Tizz.

I thought in all honesty that I probably wouldn't; at least, not physically. All the same, I was sorry I'd automatically assumed that Tizz had been at fault. All she'd been doing was standing up for Mum. It was so unfair to say that Mum was a benefit scrounge! Right up until the end of last year she'd worked every day at Chicken 'n' Chips, just down the road. It's where she'd met Nikki, her so-called *friend*. She'd only stopped working when Chicken 'n' Chips had gone broke and had to close down. If they hadn't have closed, she'd have still been there. She'd tried to find another job. She'd been for loads of interviews. But she had to tell people she was taking medication, and what she was taking it for, and we thought perhaps it frightened them cos nobody ever offered her anything.

Rather nervously, I asked Tizz if any of the teachers had seen what happened.

"Dunno," said Tizz. "Don't care. Not going back."

What???

"But you've got to!" I said.

"If I go back," said Tizz, "I'll kill her."

"But what about Sammy? She needs you to take her in! And bring her home."

"I'll take her in," said Tizz. "I'll even bring her home. But I am *not going back.*"

I couldn't seem to find the energy to argue with her. All I could hope was that she'd simmer down over the weekend and be a bit more reasonable. Otherwise, what could I do? I couldn't force her to go to school.

"Know what?" I said. "I don't care. I don't care about anything any more."

"Me neither," said Tizz. "What are we going to eat?"

"Dunno," I said. "Dunno what there is."

Tizz opened the cupboard. "*Beans. Spaghetti. Soup.*"

I shrugged. "Whatever."

"Else there's cornflakes," said Tizz, "'cept we don't have any milk."

"What?" That shook me. "No milk?" How could we possibly be out of milk?

"All got drunk," said Tizz.

"When?"

"I dunno."

"I mean, when did you find out?"

"Dunno. Last night?"

"Why didn't you tell me?" I glared at her, exasperated. "I could have got some on the way home! You'll have to go up the road."

"What, now?" said Tizz.

"Yes! We can't be without milk."

"Why can't we?"

"Cos we need it for the cornflakes."

"Why?"

I said, "You want to eat cornflakes *dry*?"

"Don't want to eat cornflakes at all," said Tizz.

"You will when you're starving," I said.

I went to the cupboard and groped around for the empty yogurt pot which I'd used for hiding what was left of our emergency fund. To my horror, all it had in it was a 50p piece. Where had the rest of it gone?

And then I looked at Tizz, and I knew. She hadn't been stealing things, she'd raided the yoghurt pot. Which in a way was just the same as stealing. No wonder she didn't want me sending her up the road to buy milk! She knew we didn't have enough money left.

I said, "Tizz, how *could* you?"

She tossed her head, defiantly. "At least I didn't spend it on rotting veg! And anyway," she added, "there's not long to go."

She meant that it would soon be Tuesday. The day she had marked on the calendar. The day that Mum was due back. But just because Mum had been away for ten days last time didn't mean she was only going to be away for ten days this time. She could be anywhere. With anyone. Doing anything.

I tried to imagine how it might have happened. Mum meeting someone. Thinking – as she had thought so many times before – that this was The One. Whizzing off in a whirl of excitement, all else forgotten.

I'd been too young, that first time, for Mum to tell me where she had been, or what she'd been doing. If she even remembered. She'd said once that when she was in one of her Big Happies it was like life was exploding all around her. Like a fireworks display, everything bright and flashing.

Another time she'd said it was like being on a roller coaster, racing along at a thousand miles per hour, totally out of control and not able to get off. Frightening, I'd have thought, but Mum said that while it was actually happening it was exhilarating. You felt on top of the world, capable of anything. But with life rushing past at the speed of light you just couldn't keep a grip on all the ordinary, everyday things. Not even the things that meant most to you in the whole world, such as your children. They just became a blur, like you were seeing them in the far, dim distance, through a thick mist.

I took the 50p out of the yoghurt pot and threw it across the table.

"Here," I said. "Take it! You might just as well, you took all the rest."

"I really don't see," said Tizz, "why you're making such a fuss."

Fuss? What fuss? I wasn't making any fuss!

"We can live without milk for just a few days. *Can't* we?"

I didn't say anything to this.

"Rube?" Tizz looked at me, suspiciously. "*Rubee?*"

I said, "Shut up! Just SHUT UP!"

"Ruby, don't cry," said Tizz. "Please don't! I'm sorry if I upset you. Please don't cry, Ruby!"

But now that I'd started, I couldn't stop. I'm not like Tizz, who never cries. I just don't cry very often. But when I do, I do it BIG TIME.

I stood by the cupboard, weeping. Tizz hovered, dabbing at me with a tissue and patting me on the shoulder. Sammy, fortunately, was in the other room.

"Mum *will* be back," said Tizz. "She will be, she will be! *Please*, Ruby—"

The sound of someone knocking at the front door made her break off. We looked at each other in alarm. Who could it be? Not Her Upstairs again!

"*Mu-u-u-m!*"

We heard Sammy give a howl and go scampering into the hall.

"Don't answer it!" shrieked Tizz. "Look and see who it is!"

It couldn't be Mum; Mum would use her key. Unless, of course…

Me and Tizz exchanged glances.

"It could be," whispered Tizz.

My tears had dried up as if by magic. We stood, straining our ears, waiting for Sammy's joyous cry.

But the cry never came. Instead, Sammy trailed slowly

back, sucking on her thumb. We waited for her to say something. I could feel my heart thudding and banging. In the end, Tizz could bear it no longer. She said, "Well?"

Sammy spoke without taking her thumb out of her mouth. Her eyes were large and apprehensive.

"It'th a man," she said.

"What sort of man?!" I pulled her thumb out of her mouth. "Not a policeman?"

"A black man," said Sammy.

"Is he wearing a uniform?"

Slowly, Sammy shook her head.

"Could be plain clothes," said Tizz.

But how would we know?

CHAPTER NINE

The knocking came again. Louder, this time. Sammy's eyes grew big and frightened. I looked at Tizz. Suppose it really was the police? What should we do?

The knocker thundered and crashed. If it *was* the police and we didn't answer, they might break the door down. I swallowed.

"I s'ppose we'd better go and see."

"Just look," said Tizz.

Together, we crept into the hall.

"You stay there," I told Sammy; but she had to come creeping after us.

I was about to peer through the narrow window at the side of the door when the letter box flap was pushed up and a familiar voice echoed down the hallway: "Anyone there? Debs? You there?"

"Oh!" Relief flooded over me. "It's Cal!"

Tizz flung open the door. Cal stood there, grinning. Long and lanky, his hair in dreadlocks. Tizz hurled herself at him.

"Hallo, hallo!" He swept her up and swung her round, then did the same to me. "Oh, my, aren't we grown? Last time I saw you, you was all little an' tiny!"

I said, "That was ages ago. I'm in Year eight, now."

"I believe you," said Cal. "Who's this hiding away, sucking her thumb?"

Sammy immediately tucked herself behind me, peering out from behind my legs.

"She probably doesn't remember you," I said. "She was too young."

"And now she's a huge great girl of... what? Five?"

Sammy took her thumb out of her mouth. She said, "I'm Sammy and I'm six."

"You never are!" said Cal.

"I am so," said Sammy.

Tizz said, "It was her birthday just yesterday."

"Is that a fact? We'll have to see if we can't do something about that! Meanwhile—" Cal glanced round the hall. "Where's your mum? Is she here?"

Sammy put her thumb back in her mouth. Me and Tizz each waited for the other to say something. Neither of us did.

"She all right?" said Cal.

"She..." I swallowed.

"She what?"

"She's disappeared!" Tizz spat the words out,

looking at me defiantly. "She's gone off and we don't know where she is, and —" she hiccupped — "we haven't got any money and the food's all running out and—"

"Hey, hey!" Cal put an arm round Tizz's shoulders. "I'm here now, you'll be OK. You're safe! Let's all go and sit ourselves down and you can tell me what happened. Don't worry, don't worry! We'll get things sorted! Cal sank on to the sofa with Sammy on his lap, me and Tizz on either side. "So... when did your mum actually take off?"

"Ages ago! Saturday."

"You've been on your own since Saturday? What have you been eating?"

Proudly I told him that we had gone to Tesco and bought as much as we could with what little money we had been able to find.

"But it's nearly all gone," said Tizz. "Even the emergency fund!"

"That's cos of you going and spending it," I said.

"Pardon me," said Tizz, "you were the one that bought all those rotten vegetables. I j—"

"Ssh!" Cal put a finger to his lips. "Don't let's fall out. Do I take it you haven't told anyone?"

I said, "No, cos you know what'd happen? Same as last time. They'd put us in a home!"

"Yeah." Cal nodded. "I remember."

He hadn't been there that first time, but he'd heard all about it. Mum had never kept any secrets from Cal.

"Thing is—" He looked at us, gravely. "We can't let it go on too long. If she's been missing since Saturday... that's nearly a week."

Quick as a flash, Tizz said, "It was ten days last time! But then she came back. Like she will again! I've marked it on the calendar... Tuesday. That's when she'll come back!"

Cal said, "Sure, baby! Sure!"

It worried me that he didn't sound totally convinced. More like he was simply saying it to keep us happy.

"She wouldn't just forget us," I said.

"Of course she wouldn't! She loves you. It's just…" Cal's voice trailed off. "Tell me exactly what happened," he said. "You got home and she wasn't here?"

I said, "It was when we woke up."

"Sunday morning," said Tizz.

"So she actually went off… when? Saturday evening?"

"With Nikki," I said.

"Oh." Cal pulled a face. He obviously remembered Nikki.

"Nikki and her boyfriend."

"Who's total *rubbish*," said Tizz.

Cal said yes, he could imagine.

"We went to the Carnival," I said, "and Mum spent all her money and Nikki just kept, like, egging her on. Then in the evening they all went off clubbing. But Mum didn't have hardly any money left!"

"She did leave a message," said Tizz. "She didn't do that last time."

"It's still on the answerphone," I said. "D'you want to hear it?"

We all sat in silence, listening to Mum's voice.

Darlings, darlings! Love you, darlings! Thinking of you! Always thinking of you! Don't worry, my darlings! We'll have lemonade sky! Lemonade sky! I promise you, poppets! That's what we'll have! Lemonade sky!…

For a long time, at the end, nobody said anything. Cal was looking troubled.

"She sounds a bit hyper," he said. "She not been taking her meds?"

"I try to watch her," I said. "I do, honestly! But sometimes she says she's taken them and then it turns out she hasn't, and—"

"I know, baby, I know!" Cal hugged me to him. "You can't be expected to shoulder all the responsibility. Believe me, I used to have the exact same problem. The exact same! She'd swear blind she'd taken them."

"It's not her fault," I said. "She hates them!"

"What we can't understand," said Tizz, "is what's with this lemonade sky?"

Cal said, "Yeah, that's something that's always puzzled me. She's mentioned it before. Whenever I tried asking her about it, she said she couldn't remember. It obviously meant something to her at some time, but I never discovered what."

"Lemonade pie," chirped Sammy, suddenly brightening.

"Sounds good," said Cal. "Listen, before we decide what to do… you kids must be starving. How about we all go up the road and have a pizza?"

"When you first knocked on the door," said Tizz, as we left the flat, "we thought you might be a policeman."

"Or Her Upstairs," I said.

"We didn't think he could be Her Upstairs! How could *he* be *her*?" Tizz's voice was full of scorn. She was just trying to impress Cal. She always thinks of herself as being superior, just cos in some ways she is cleverer than I am.

"What I meant," I said, "I meant before we sent Sammy to have a look."

"So if that's what you meant," said Tizz, "that's what you should have said. I was talking about *after* Sammy had had a look."

"You said when he first knocked at the door!"

"I s—"

"Now, now, you two!" Cal wagged a finger. "That's enough of that. Behave yourselves or I'll send you both back and just me and Sammy will have a pizza."

We subsided, with mutterings from Tizz.

"As a matter of interest," said Cal, "what would you have done if I had been a policeman? Ruby? You're the one in charge. What would you have done?"

Tizz made a scoffing sound. "She'd have gone and opened the door!"

"And you reckon that would have been wrong?"

"Yes, cos how would you know if someone really was a policeman? Only if you saw their card, and how could you see their card unless you'd opened the door? By which time," said Tizz, with an air of horrible smugness, "it'd be too late!"

"Unless they were police in uniform," I said.

"Still got to see their card," said Tizz.

I said, "You think people are going to dress up and *pretend*?"

"They do," said Tizz. "They do it all the time! Pretend to be police just so's you'll let them in and th—"

"Enough!" Cal clapped both hands to his ears. He looked down at Sammy. "Are they always like this?"

Sammy gazed doubtfully from me to Tizz.

"We're not *always*," I said. "It's just—" I broke off, suddenly feeling that I might burst into tears.

"It's cos of Mum not being here," said Tizz. "Ruby's got all bossy. She thinks she can tell us what to do!"

"She is the oldest," said Cal. He put his arm round me and I felt the tears well up in my eyes. "I'm sure she's done her best."

"Yeah." Tizz aimed a kick at a stray lager can rolling about on the pavement. "I guess."

"Well, I have!" I said.

Tizz scowled. "I know you have. Don't keep on!"

Slowly, as we ate our pizzas, I began to cheer up. It is very difficult to be cheerful when your stomach is flapping. But now that Cal was here, and now that I was getting all nicely filled up with pizza (followed by ice cream, followed by milkshake) I was starting to feel a bit braver. Mum *would* come back. Of course she would! And in future I would take better care of her. I would be the keeper of the medicine cabinet! I would make sure that she really did take her medicine every day. I wouldn't let her wriggle out of it! When she tried saying, "Oh, Ruby, later," or, "Yes, yes, darling, just leave it there," I would stand firm. I wouldn't move till she'd swallowed it.

I announced this as Cal was drinking his coffee and we were slurping our milk shakes. Cal said, "Way to go! You gotta be firm."

"This is it," said Tizz. "You've let her get away with things." And then, maybe sensing that I was about to clonk her on the head with the tomato sauce bottle, she quickly added, "When Mum gets back we'll *both* look after her."

"Right. Shared responsibility," said Cal. "Who, by the way, is this Upstairs person you were talking about?"

"Her Upstairs," said Tizz. "She's a mean, spiteful, nosy old woman that's always poking and prying and complaining about Mum borrowing stuff and not giving it back and not putting the rubbish out properly. Like it matters!"

"Ruby?" Cal turned to me. "Is she really that bad?"

"She's a bit interfering," I said. "She keeps wanting to know where Mum is."

"What have you told her?"

"Just that she's out. But I don't think she believes it. She wants to come and complain about something and she's getting, like, really suspicious? Like she thinks Mum is hiding from her."

Cal nodded. "I get the picture. I guess your mum does have a bit of a knack for upsetting people."

"She does not!" roared Tizz; but I knew that Cal

was right. Not that Mum *wants* to upset anyone. When she's on what she calls an even keel, like when she takes her meds and doesn't get hyper or sink into depression, she's really very considerate.

"I guess tomorrow," said Cal, as we left the restaurant, "we're going to have to work out what to do."

"'Bout what?" said Tizz.

"About you. About your mum. You can't go on living here on your own."

"But we're not *on* our own," said Tizz. "You're here!"

"And what do you imagine Her Upstairs would have to say about that?"

"Don't see why she should say anything! Don't see it's any of her business."

"What, with no sign of your mum and a strange man suddenly appearing?"

"We could say you're our dad!" said Tizz.

There was a pause.

"You could say it," agreed Cal.

But who would believe it?

Rather desperately Tizz cried, "Our *adopted* dad! You could be our *adopted* dad!"

I slipped my hand into Cal's. "I wish you were," I whispered.

I was so relieved when I went to bed that night, knowing that Cal was going to be there, just a short distance away, in Mum's room. For the first time in ages I fell asleep the minute I closed my eyes. I slept all through the night! I think Sammy must have done, too, cos she actually stayed in her own bed. *And* she didn't make any damp patches.

I had a bit of a panic when I woke up next morning, thinking that Cal might not still be there. Suppose his itchy feet had made him suddenly take off?

I went tiptoeing out in my nightie. The door of Mum's room was ajar. I could tell the bed had been slept in, but there was no sign of Cal. And then I heard the sound of the fridge being opened and went rushing into the kitchen to find Cal peering in dismay at the empty shelves.

"You really are out of everything, aren't you?" he said.

Anxiously, cos I didn't want him thinking I'd let Tizz and Sammy starve, I pointed out that we did still have a few tins left.

"Yeah, I saw. Baked beans!" He pulled a face. "Don't fancy them for breakfast. I'd better go up the road and get something. That little shop still there on the corner?"

I said, "Yes, but shall I go?"

"No, no, you stay here," said Cal. "I'm already up and dressed." He started for the door, then stopped and looked at me. "Is there a problem?"

My face must have given me away.

"You will come back?" I quavered.

"Oh, baby, of course I will! Trust me." He tilted my chin with the tip of a finger. "You do trust me, don't you?"

I nodded.

"Well, then! Go and get the others up and I'll be back before you know it."

"Hope he doesn't bump into Her Upstairs," said Tizz, when I told her that Cal was out buying stuff for breakfast. "Would have been better," she said, "if you'd gone."

"I did offer," I said.

"Her Upstairs is enough to put anyone off. He might decide not to come back." Tizz's lower lip trembled slightly. "You should have gone with him!"

I knew she wasn't really accusing me. She was just frightened that Cal would disappear, like Mum, and we'd be on our own again.

"Let's go and lay the table," I said, "and make it all nice."

In one of the kitchen drawers we found a tablecloth we'd completely forgotten about, and some old paper napkins that had been there forever. We set them out on the table, with knives and spoons, and plates and bowls and mugs.

"That looks really good," said Tizz.

"Now we just need to clean the kitchen up," I said.

I used the dustpan and brush for the floor, while Tizz scrubbed at the sink till it was bright and sparkling. It had never occurred to us to do any housework-type stuff and I'd suddenly become aware that the whole place was a bit disgusting. Plus it stopped us thinking too much about what would happen if Cal didn't come back. I was sure he would; but suppose he didn't?

Oh, but he did! Tizz and I went catapulting into the hall to greet him.

"What's all this?" he said. "I've only been gone twenty minutes!"

"Has he bringed food?" Sammy had already taken her seat at the table. She seemed to have accepted that Cal was now in charge and would provide us with all our needs. I told her not to be so rude and greedy, but Cal just laughed.

"She certainly has her priorities right. Here you go! Unpack this lot."

"Eggs!" Sammy squeaked, excitedly. "We can have bald eggs!"

"Boiled," I said.

"Bald," said Sammy. "And fingers!"

It was the first proper breakfast we'd had since I couldn't hardly remember. Boiled eggs, toast and butter, toast and marmalade, cereal, milk… Tizz said it was like a banquet.

After we'd finished, Cal said we had to talk. He sent Sammy off to watch television, while him and me and Tizz sat round the table to sort out, as Cal said, what we were going to do. I didn't see why we had to do anything.

"Can't we just stay here?" I said. "Wait till Mum gets back?"

Gravely, Cal shook his head. He said, "I'm afraid that's not really an option."

"Why not?" Tizz sat up, very straight and aggressive. "So long as you stay here with us!"

"You know I can't do that," said Cal. He said it very gently, like he really regretted it, but I just had this feeling there wasn't going to be anything we could do to persuade him.

Tizz's face had gone all puckered. "Why can't you stay with us?"

"Cos I'm not your dad. Not even your adopted one."

"What does that matter?"

"It matters," said Cal.

"Doesn't matter to me," said Tizz. She was blinking, rather furiously. Cal stretched out a hand and squeezed one of hers.

"Listen, baby, I'm not going to desert you! But we need to find somewhere safe for you. Just till your mum gets back."

That was when alarm bells started ringing. "We're not going into care," I said. "Cal, please! Please! You can't do that to us!"

"Sooner run away," said Tizz, knuckling at her eyes.

Cal sat for a while in silence, a frown creasing his forehead.

"This Nikki," he said. "Do you have a number for her?"

I shook my head. "Mum's probably got it on her phone."

"I take it you have tried calling your mum?"

"She's switched her phone off," said Tizz. "Either that or it needs recharging."

"Or it's run out of money."

"So how about an address?"

"For Nikki? We haven't got one."

"Not even sure where she lives," said Tizz.

"And anyway," I said, "we couldn't go and live with her. She's an idiot!"

"Yeah, I remember," said Cal. "I just thought she might have some idea where your mum could have gone. What about the place they used to work? Chicken 'n' Chips, or whatever it was?"

"It closed," said Tizz.

"Hm." Cal drummed his fingers on the table. "In that case, I wonder…"

CHAPTER TEN

Me and Tizz sat waiting. What was Cal going to say?

"I wonder if there's any way we could get in touch with your nan?"

Our nan? We stared at him. We didn't even know we had a nan!

"You never hear from her?" said Cal.

Silently, we shook our heads.

"Your mum never mentions her?"

A faint memory came back to me. "I think she might have done," I said, "one time when I was little and I was, like, refusing to eat my sprouts, or something."

"You still do," said Tizz.

"I know, I hate them!"

"And Mum always lets you off."

"Yes, cos she says she doesn't believe in forcing a person to eat stuff they really don't like, but *her* mum used to make her sit there until she'd cleaned her plate. That's what she told me."

"Sounds about right," said Cal. "I always gathered she was a bit of a martinet."

I looked at him, doubtfully. I didn't know what a martinet was, but it didn't sound like it was anything good. Tizz, boldly, said, "I never heard Mum say that, and what's a mart'net?"

"Someone who's very strict," said Cal. And then, catching sight of my face, he quickly added that it could just have been Mum's interpretation. "She'd have been a handful, you can bet."

Tizz, in her aggressive manner, immediately demanded to know how. "*How* would Mum have been a handful?"

"Playing up?" said Cal. "Acting out? Never doing what she was told."

I thought privately that it sounded a bit like Tizz, but I didn't say so. I wanted to hear more about this unknown nan. Already I was starting to not like the sound of her.

"I just met her the once," said Cal. "Remember when you lived in Portsmouth? Some dreadful dump down near the Docks. D'you remember?"

I did, vaguely, though we had lived in lots of places since.

"I don't," said Tizz.

"You were too young. And Sammy wasn't even born. Anyway, this woman suddenly turned up when your mum was out, saying she was Deb's mum, so I let her in and said she was welcome to wait, and I remember she sat there looking like she'd stepped into a pig sty and got pig muck on her. *Ugh*!"

Cal gave a little high-pitched shriek and a ladylike shudder and crossed his legs. Both Tizz and me giggled.

"Mind you," he said, "I can't honestly blame her. Your mum was going through one of her bad patches. The place really was a bit like a pig sty. I was pretty glad to get out of it. I guess I should have stuck around, but—"

"You had itchy feet," I said. I didn't want Cal feeling guilty.

"Is that what your mum says? I've got itchy feet? Well, I guess she's right. But I should have stayed on. I was really worried about you kids, how your mum was going to cope. I kind of assumed, now your nan had turned up, that she'd take care of things. See, I'd really just dropped by to say hallo, and – then I was off. I didn't stay around long enough to check how things worked out. It was only later, like months later, I found out what had happened. Seems your mum and your gran had a big bust up. A real set-to. You know what your mum's like when she loses it. She said your nan was an interfering old – well, I won't say what she called her, but apparently your mum told her to get out of her life and stay out, and as far as I'm aware that's exactly what she did. You say she's never been in touch?"

"No, and if she had," said Tizz, "I wouldn't want to speak to her! Not if she upset Mum."

I loved Tizz for being so loyal, but I knew that when Mum was going through one of her bad patches it could make her a bit unreasonable.

"I reckon what it was," said Cal, "she thought your nan was having a go at her. Which she probably was. And that's one thing your mum can't stand. I shouldn't be surprised if it's one of the reasons she moved. So your nan wouldn't be able to trace you."

"Did we ever meet her?" I said. "Cos I don't remember."

Cal said no, we'd both been at school.

"How old were we?" I said.

"Well… when did you move to Southampton? Some years ago. You must have been about… five?"

And now I was twelve. "If she hasn't bothered to get in touch after all this time," I said, "she obviously doesn't want to know."

"That doesn't necessarily have to be true," said Cal. "If she didn't have your new address, what was she supposed to do?"

"She could have hired a private detective," said Tizz. "If she'd really wanted to find us, that's what she'd have done."

"Well, yeah, OK, maybe. But if your mum gave her a load of mouth—"

"If Mum was rude to her," said Tizz, "she must have deserved it!"

"But she is still your nan. We're going to have to try and find her."

My heart sank. "Do we really have to?" I said. "Can't we just wait for Mum to come back? I know you have itchy feet, but it'd only be for a few days and then you could go off again."

"Baby, I'm not going anywhere," said Cal. "But I don't

think we can take it for granted that your mum's just going to turn up on the doorstep. She might, she might! I'm not saying she won't. But remember I asked you what you'd have done if I'd been the police? It might be time that we actually went to them."

"The *police*?"

"We might have to. Your mum's missing. We need to find her."

Angrily Tizz said, "She's not missing! She's just doing her own thing, like she did last time."

"If she's not been taking her meds," said Cal, gently, "she probably doesn't know *what* she's doing."

I knew, deep down, that Cal was right. "But if we go to the police," I wailed, "they'll say Mum's neglecting us and they'll take us into care!"

"That's why we have to find your gran. Now, let's get our thinking caps on! *My* thinking cap. I'm trying to remember anything your mum might have told me about her." Cal stood up and began pacing the room. "One thing I remember, she was fraffly fraffly."

"What's fraffly fraffly?"

"Fraffly posh, dontcha know? A bit like the Queen… except she barked a lot."

"Like a royal corgi," I said.

"Yeah! Good one." Cal laughed. "Like a royal corgi. Oh, and yeah, it's coming back to me… she *was* like the Queen. She was horsey! Ran a riding stables. Somewhere in the New Forest. Place called…" He tapped a finger against his teeth. "Began with a B… Black – Brack – Brock – Brockenhurst! That was it. Your mum once told me how she was brought up there. They moved there after your granddad died. Let's Google it! Riding stables in Brockenhurst. Where's your computer?"

"It doesn't work," I said. It hadn't worked for months. Probably because it had been second hand and already worn out when we got it.

Cal clicked his tongue, impatiently. "OK! Let's try the telephone book."

"Haven't got one," said Tizz.

"We have," I said. "We've got a yellow one."

"Yellow pages," said Cal. "That'll do."

I scampered off to get it, pleased that I had remembered and Tizz hadn't.

"I bet it's out of date," said Tizz.

She obviously wanted it to be. She was just *so-o-o* jealous! But Cal said it didn't matter if it was a few years old.

"We know your nan was round six, seven years ago, so at least, with any luck, it'll give us a number."

"But she mightn't still be there!"

"In that case there'll be new people running the place and the chances are they'll be able to tell us where she's gone."

"If they know," muttered Tizz.

"We can but try."

Tizz went, "Huh!" It occurred to me that she didn't actually want Cal to find this unknown nan. I wasn't sure that I did, either. But I meekly handed over the directory, all tattered and torn and scribbled over, and watched anxiously as Cal leafed through the pages.

"There's three that seem likely. Number one, *New Forest Riding School*. Let's give it a go… OK, it's ringing… Hallo, good morning, I wonder if you can help me. I'm looking for a Mrs Tindall?"

I held my breath. I think Tizz must have been holding hers, as well, cos she let it out in a great *whoosh!* as Cal shook his head.

"Right. One down, two to go… let's try the next one. *Premier Stables and Livery*… Yes, hallo! I'd like to speak with a Mrs Tindall?"

There was a pause. I could hear a voice speaking at the other end, but I couldn't hear what it was saying. Then Cal said, "Thank you very much, that's fine. I'll do that. OK!" He turned to us, triumphant. "Call back in about half an hour. She should be there."

I couldn't think what to say. It was Tizz who burst out with, "Why is her name the same as Mum's?"

"Tindall? Well—" Cal seemed puzzled by the question. "Your mum's her daughter."

"But *Mum* is Mrs Tindall."

She meant that Tindall was Mum's married name. The name of the man that had been my dad. It had to be. I knew it wasn't the name of Tizz's dad, cos that was Pike. Andy Pike. And Sammy's dad had been O'Leary. So it had to be mine!

But Cal was shaking his head. "Your mum always kept her maiden name," he said.

Tizz wrinkled her forehead. "Why would she do that? 'Stead of a married one?"

Oh, please! I rolled my eyes. Tizz saw me, and grew red.

"You mean, she never got married?"

"People don't always," said Cal. "Lots of people don't. Not just your mum."

I wondered, in that case, what *my* dad's name had been. I'd never thought to ask. I'd just automatically assumed it was Tindall.

Tizz said, "Her Upstairs always calls Mum Mrs. She says –" Tizz folded her arms – "*Mrs* Tindall, I have cause to ask you *yet again* not to put your rubbish bin where mine is supposed to go."

I had to giggle, cos she really did sound like Her Upstairs. Even Cal couldn't help grinning.

"Let's just hope we don't bump into her before I take you down to your nan's!"

"Do you really think she'll want us?" I said.

"I'm hoping so."

"Suppose she doesn't?"

"We'll cross that bridge when we come to it," said Cal.

"S'ppose *we* don't want to?" Tizz put the question, fiercely. "S'ppose we'd rather just stay here and wait for Mum? You don't have to stay with us if you don't want to. You didn't before, and we managed all right. You could just lend us some money and we could look after ourselves, same as we've been doing. We're not useless!"

"You're not," agreed Cal. "Ruby's done a splendid job, holding things together, but it's not fair expecting her to go on doing it."

"She doesn't mind! She likes bossing us around. Don't you?" Tizz jabbed at me, daring me to say that I didn't. "Tell him! You enjoy it."

I hesitated. I didn't want to go and live with this strange horsey barking person any more than Tizz, but I wasn't sure how much longer I could go on fighting battles, trying to get her and Sammy to do what they were told, always having to worry about whether there was going to be enough food, or whether someone was going to discover about Mum.

"Oh, you are such a wimp!" cried Tizz. She sounded thoroughly disgusted.

"Let's not get too worked up," said Cal. "We'll see what happens when I speak to your nan. Why don't you two go and keep Sammy company?"

"Why?" said Tizz, immediately suspicious. "What are you going to do?"

"I have one or two things I have to take care of."

"You're not going to call the police?"

There was a shrill note of alarm in Tizz's voice.

Soothingly, Cal said that he wasn't. "Not before I've had a word with your nan. I wouldn't do it without telling you, I promise."

"He shouldn't do it at all," grumbled Tizz, as we wandered in to the other room to sit with Sammy. "It's not up to him! She's our mum."

I didn't say, "But he's a grown up," cos I don't think grown-ups can always be relied on to make the right decisions, simply because they are grown up. They're just the ones with the power. But a bit of me did reluctantly feel that Cal might be right. We had no idea where Mum was or what kind of trouble she might be in. Going to the police was a bit scary, but after all they are supposed to be there to *help* people. Not just to arrest them.

"Wonder what he's doing?" said Tizz, when we'd sat patiently for half an hour. "D'you think he's ringing her?"

"Dunno."

"D'you think we should go and listen?"

I was tempted, but it would have seemed horribly

like spying. Like Cal was someone we couldn't trust. I said this to Tizz, but she angrily reminded me that it was us he was ringing about.

"We've got a right to know what's happening!"

"He'll tell us," I said.

"But I want to hear what's going on. I want to know what he's saying!"

"So go and eavesdrop."

Tizz started up, then sank back down.

"Both of us," she said.

"No." I wriggled myself deeper into the corner of the sofa. "I think we should wait till he's done it."

Tizz made a huffing sound.

"I'm not stopping *you*," I said.

But it seemed that I was, cos she huddled into the other corner of the sofa and sat there scowling and hugging her legs up to her chin, looking like some kind of malevolent garden gnome.

"Know what?" I said. "If you went and sat in the backyard like that you'd do a great job scaring the pigeons away. Her Upstairs might even give you a tip."

Her Upstairs was forever complaining about the pigeons. She said they were no better than vermin and ought to be exterminated.

So I'll thank you, Mrs Tindall, to stop encouraging them!

Personally I think pigeons have as much right to exist as we do, but Her Upstairs has this mad bloodlust thing where she just wants to kill. Rats, mice, foxes, geese. Omigod, she hates geese! She says they make a disgusting mess all over the park. She s—

"OK!" The door suddenly opened and Cal appeared. We swung round to face him.

"Have you done it?" said Tizz.

"I have, and everything's sorted. Your nan's going to look after you till your mum comes back. I said I'd take you down to her right away. Oh, now, come on!" Our faces had obviously fallen. "You know it's the right thing to do. At least you'll be safe and well cared for."

"But she barks," said Tizz. "And she's fraffly fraffly!"

"She's your nan," said Cal. "To be honest, she didn't sound that bad. I mean, yeah, sure, she barks a bit, but when I told her about your mum she didn't hesitate. She said straight off that you should go to her."

Tizz was scowling. One of her particularly ferocious scowls that scrunched up her whole face.

"Seems like we don't get to have any say in the matter."

"That's what comes of being kids," said Cal.

Tizz gulped. "It's not funny!"

"Oh, baby, I know it isn't." Cal tried to put his arm round her, but she moved away, stiff and furious. "Nobody's saying it's funny. Not for you, not for your mum. But one thing you don't want, and that's to go into care. Believe me, I've been there! I was in care till I was sixteen years old. I'm not going to let that happen to you, which is why I'm taking you down to your nan. With any luck you'll only be there for a day or two, and then your mum'll be back. Now, let's go see what you need to pack. Ruby! You're in charge."

We could only find one battered suitcase, so we had to cram lots of stuff into carrier bags. Sammy wanted to know where we were going.

"Are we going to find Mum?"

I said no, we were going to stay with our nan. "Just until Mum gets back."

Sammy thought about this for a while, frowning as she watched me stuff knickers and T-shirts into a bag.

"What's a nan?" she said.

I found it hard to believe she didn't know what a nan was.

"It's Mum's mum," I said.

Sammy seemed confused. She said she didn't know that Mum had a mum.

"Oh, for goodness' sake!" snapped Tizz. "Everybody has a mum."

"Imagine," I said, "you're going to meet your nan for the very first time. It'll be fun!"

Tizz snorted. I sent her a warning glare.

"Is she nice?" said Sammy.

"You bet," said Cal. "She's really eager to see you! She keeps horses," he added. "If you're good, she might even let you ride one."

At this, Sammy burst into tears and said she didn't want to ride one, she just wanted Mum! Poor Cal looked quite crestfallen. I felt really sorry for him. He was trying so hard, and we were all being so ungracious. I told Sammy rather sharply to dry her eyes and stop behaving like a baby.

"Cal's taking us on holiday! You should be grateful."

If Tizz had made one of her smart-mouth remarks I really think I would have thrown a pair of knickers at her. But she just picked up her carrier bag and snarled, "What are we waiting for? Let's just *go*."

"OK," said Cal. "If you're ready."

I was worried in case Mum might turn up and wonder where we were, but Cal said he'd written her a note.

"In any case," he said, "I'll be coming straight back after I've dropped you off."

He promised that he would stick around as long as was necessary.

"I won't be going anywhere until your mum's safely back. In the meanwhile you're only half an hour away, and we can always talk on the phone, so don't feel you've been abandoned."

"But suppose you get itchy feet?" I said.

Cal laughed. "Just have to scratch them, I guess!"

CHAPTER ELEVEN

I had always imagined someone's Nan as being old and grey-haired, dressed in old lady clothes. All baggy and saggy. Shapeless cardies and stretchy pants. Pale pink or blue. Definitely not smart. But I'd also imagined that a nan would be someone warm and soft. A person you could go to for cuddles. That's what I'd imagined.

Mum's mum wasn't any of those things. For a start, she wasn't what you would call old. Not *old* old. And her clothes weren't baggy or saggy. She was wearing a striped shirt, not a cardie, and instead of stretchy pants she had on a really cool pair of jeans. Ones I wouldn't have minded for myself.

Above all, she wasn't either warm or soft. She was slim and kind of tough-looking, with the same red hair as Mum only not pretty and curly like Mum's. She wore it scraped back, very tight, from her face. And no make-up *at all*. Mum didn't wear very much, but she did like a touch of eye shadow and lipstick. I had the feeling that this woman (I found it really difficult to think of her as our nan) would probably regard make-up as too frivolous. Definitely *not* someone you would go to for cuddles.

Her house was a bit like her. Very clean and scrubbed and tidy. We were not used to clean and scrubbed, and Mum had never been a great one for tidiness, so that my heart went plummeting and I wondered how we would get on. I saw *trouble*, 'specially with Tizz. I couldn't imagine this woman putting up with Tizz and her temper.

When she came to the door to greet us, a great barking dog came with her. She said, "Piper, pipe down! Take no notice of him, he's quite harmless."

The dog stopped barking and gave us a big wolfish grin, which I didn't like the look of. Sammy cringed behind me, clutching at my legs. Only bold Tizz stood her ground. She said, "Hallo, dog," and held out a hand. The dog immediately launched itself at her, which made Sammy scream. The woman snapped, "Oh, for goodness' sake, he's not going to hurt you! He's a Staffie. Softest dog in the world. All he wants is a hug."

Didn't look to me like that was what he wanted, but Tizz had both arms round his neck and seemed to be *kissing* him. The woman nodded, approvingly.

"That's better! Let him get to know you. Now, then, who do we have? You must be Ruby?" I nodded, keeping a wary eye on the dog. "The little one is... I forget! Remind me."

"This is Sammy," said Cal.

"Short for Samantha, I presume? And this is… Tirzah?"

"Tizz," I said.

"Tizz? What kind of a name is Tizz?"

If it came to that, what kind of a name was Tirzah? Mum only chose it cos it was the name of someone in a book she happened to be reading at the time.

"Well, come in, come in! I'm your grandmother, as you obviously know. You may call me Gran, or Grandma, whichever you prefer, but I give you due warning, I will not answer to either Nan or Nana."

Cal pulled a face, like he was a naughty boy that had been told off. Tizz said, "I like Gran."

"Then Gran it shall be. Come!"

She led the way into a big airy room, all painted white, with oceans of carpet and enormous windows looking on to a garden that seemed to stretch for ever. Cal and me sat in armchairs, with Sammy perched on my lap. Tizz bounced down on to a sofa. The dog leapt up beside her. I waited for the woman – *Gran* – to shout at him to get off, but she seemed to think a dog being on the sofa was quite normal.

"Now," she said, "before we go any further, let me see if I've understood correctly." She turned to Cal. "You say Deborah's been missing since Sunday?"

"Right. She went off clubbing Saturday evening and didn't come back. But she did leave a message on the answerphone."

"Saying what, exactly?"

"Well…" Cal looked a bit uncertain. I rushed in to help him.

"She said she loved us and we'd all have lemonade sky."

"You'd have *what?*"

"L-lemonade sky?"

"What is that supposed to mean?"

"It means she's coming back," said Tizz. "We'll have lemonade sky *when she gets back.*"

"And in the meantime… ?"

We all looked at one another.

"Where exactly has she gone?"

Cal shook his head. "She didn't say."

"So you have absolutely no idea where she is or who she might be with?"

Gran's eyes bored into each one of us in turn. I shifted, uncomfortably.

"This all happened almost a week ago, and you're telling me that you haven't bothered to ring the police?"

"She'll be back!" insisted Tizz.

Gran ignored this. Rather frostily, looking at Cal, she said, "May I suggest that ringing the police is the very *first* thing you should have done?"

Now she was being unfair. I blurted out that Cal couldn't have called the police cos he wasn't there. "It was just us!"

"And if *we'd* rung them," said Tizz, "they'd have called Social Services and they'd put us in a home."

"It's what they do," I said. "They split you up."

"Which is precisely the reason you've come to me, so that you *won't* be split up."

"We didn't know you were here," said Tizz. "Not till Cal told us. We never realised we had a gran!"

"You can blame your mother for that. She made it very plain she wanted nothing more to do with me."

Very quickly, Cal said, "I'm sure she didn't mean it. She was going through a bad patch at the time."

"And whose fault was that? If she won't take her medication—"

"She does usually take it," I said.

"We try to make sure," said Tizz. "We do our best to keep an eye on her. It's just sometimes she pretends she has when she really hasn't."

"Either that or she just forgets," I said. "Or we forget," I added.

"Your mother is a grown woman," said Gran. "It shouldn't be up to you to have to keep an eye on her. It's time she learnt to be a bit more responsible. She knows perfectly well what happens if she doesn't take her medicine."

"But she hates it!" I looked at Gran, pleadingly. I couldn't bear her being angry with Mum. "She says it makes her feel like she's living in a fog."

"Sooner that than running off and leaving three young children to fend for themselves."

"Ruby's *twelve*," said Tizz. "And she's very good at looking after us."

Gran said, "That is as maybe. It's no excuse for bad parenting."

Was she saying Mum was a bad parent? I sent furious signals to Tizz, expecting her to say something. But Tizz had found a squeaky toy amongst the sofa cushions and was driving the dog into a frenzy as she squeaked it. Why wasn't she leaping to Mum's defence?

Rather desperately I said, "It's not Mum's fault! It's the bipolar."

"Yes, and it's time she learnt to cope with it," said

Gran. "Causing all this worry and upset! Tirzah, if you want to play with Piper go and do it in the garden. I'm going to call the police."

Again, I waited for Tizz to protest, but instead she snatched up the squeaky toy and went running off, through the French windows, into the garden. Piper followed her, bouncing and barking. I turned to Cal, hoping that he would say something. He just shrugged a shoulder and gave me this sheepish grin.

"Honestly, Rubes, it's for the best."

"Don't worry." Gran said it briskly. "Whatever happens, you won't be put in a home. But we can't just sit back and do nothing. Without her medication, your mother's an easy target. She could be prey to any unscrupulous person."

"You mean—" I wasn't really sure, but I needed to be clear. What was Gran actually saying? "You mean, people could, like… take advantage of her?"

"Exactly."

I swallowed. "B-bad people?"

"Not bad, necessarily. They could just be rather stupid and thoughtless."

Like Nikki. She was stupid and thoughtless. Egging Mum on, even though she knew Mum was bipolar and not always in control. Suddenly, I felt relieved that Gran was going to ring the police. They would know what to do.

That afternoon, two police people called round. A man and a woman. We told them all we could, but it wasn't very much. We just didn't know anything! Like when they asked us if we had any idea where Mum usually went clubbing, or if we had a telephone or an address for Nikki. We weren't even sure of Nikki's surname. I had this feeling that it might be Adams, but Tizz insisted it began with an M. All we knew for certain was that she'd worked with Mum in Chicken 'n' Chips.

"Is that useful?" said Tizz.

The policewoman assured us that it was.

"Even though Chicken 'n' Chips isn't there any more?"

"We still might be able to find the owner and see if he has an address he can give us. How about any other friends? Does your mum have other friends?"

Doubtfully I said, "She does know other people. They might be on her mobile."

"Do you have her mobile number?"

We didn't even have that!

"It's at home," I said. "By the side of the phone."

Why hadn't we brought it with us?

"Have you tried ringing again, after the first time?"

Tizz put a finger in her mouth. I stared, helplessly.

"I did," said Cal. "I tried yesterday and again this morning. There's no response."

The policewoman said they would get the number and give it another go. She said they would also listen to Mum's message. I wondered if perhaps they would be able to trace the call and find out where it had come from. The police can do clever things like that. Like finding the owner of Chicken 'n' Chips. Like finding Nikki. All the things they could have done ages ago if only we hadn't been too scared to call them!

I said this to Gran, and she actually gave me a bit of a hug – well, a sort of a hug – and told me not to feel bad about it.

"From all accounts, you did a splendid job just keeping things going. Now it's time to let the police take over."

Cal said he would go back to the flat and stay there in case Mum turned up. I did so want to go with him! I tried pointing out that we still had another week of school left until the summer break, but Gran said she would sort that out and Tizz added that in any case we couldn't live in the flat with just Cal to look after us cos of Her Upstairs.

"She'd start nosing about and then she'd discover Mum wasn't there."

I didn't see that it mattered any more; not now we'd told the police. But I had this feeling Tizz didn't want to go back. She'd already formed a bond with Piper and had asked Gran if we could go to the stables and if she'd be allowed to have a ride.

"*Please*, Gran, can I? *Please?*"

Gran said, "Do you know how to ride?"

Tizz said no, but she bet she could learn. "You could put me on the biggest horse you like, I wouldn't be scared! Not even if I fell off. I'd just get straight back on again!"

I thought she was being rather pushy, not to say boastful, but Gran obviously approved. She said, "Good for you! We'll see what we can arrange. Not at the weekend, because that's our busy time. Maybe Monday afternoon. How about that?"

Tizz went "Yay!" and spent the next ten minutes galloping an imaginary horse up and down the garden, with the faithful Piper at her side. It seemed he had adopted Tizz as a playmate. She was welcome to him, as far as I was concerned. I didn't want anything to do with dogs, or horses. Horses 'specially make me nervous. They are so big, and their hooves are so hard. I am always frightened they are going to kick out. I certainly wasn't going to ride one! I was secretly hoping that by Monday we'd hear that Mum had come back and we could all go home. Tizz could stay here if she wanted. Me and Sammy would rather be with Mum.

Saturday evening Cal went back to the flat. He promised to ring us immediately if he heard anything. Like if the police called round and said they'd managed to trace Nikki or the owner of Chicken 'n' Chips.

"Don't worry," he told me. "I'll be there. Gonna give those feet a good scratch if they start to get itchy!"

"What was all that about?" said Gran, after Cal had left.

I explained how Cal had these itchy feet, and that was why he couldn't ever manage to stay in one place for very long. Gran said, "That's a pity. Your mother could do with a stabilising influence in her life."

I said, "You mean, like, if Cal was to live with us all the time it would be a good thing?"

"Your mother certainly needs someone," said Gran.

Monday afternoon came and we still hadn't heard anything. Tizz was all set to go off to the stables and have her ride, but Gran said me and Sammy could stay home if we preferred.

"There's something you might like to investigate. Here!" She handed me a cardboard box that said QUALITY WINES in red letters on the side. "There's some old stuff of your mother's in there. It's been up in the attic for years, I've just never got around to doing anything with it. Have a look through, see what you can find. Anything you want to keep, you're quite welcome. The rest might as well be thrown out. Your mother's never shown any interest in it."

As soon as Gran and Tizz had driven off, me and Sammy dived into the box. I was really excited at the thought of actually finding things that had once belonged to Mum. Being able to hold them and know that all those years ago Mum had also held them. I tried explaining this to Sammy as I picked up an old moth-eaten teddy bear.

"See? This must have been Mum's when she was little. Her teddy!"

The box was like a treasure trove. There was an autograph book with coloured pages containing messages signed Grandma and Grandpa, or Mum and Dad, plus lots from people that had maybe been at school with her. Jenny, and Zoe. Pippa, Mags, Chloe, Rachel. I wondered if Mum would remember any of them. I liked the thought of her having lots of friends.

Puzzlingly, there was a baseball cap with *Go Yankees* written on it. Why would Mum have had a baseball cap? Just for fun, perhaps. I put it on and found that it fitted me. Sammy at once said that she wanted something, so I fished out a T-shirt with glittery bits all over it, and that made her happy, even though it was far too big and came down almost to her knees. I told her she could use it as a nightie. She liked that.

Another thing I found was an old school report

from when Mum was in Year eight. The same as me! It seemed she was good at English – like me! – but bad at maths and science, and totally hopeless at all forms of sport. "Poor coordination." *Just* like me!

At the bottom were comments from her class teacher: "Deborah has a good brain when she allows herself to use it. Unfortunately she lacks concentration and is somewhat unpredictable in her moods. However, she is in general a happy and cooperative child."

I felt so sad when I read that. The thought of Mum, the same age as I was now, being happy and cooperative, even if she did lack concentration, not knowing that she was going to end up bipolar, upsetting people and quarrelling with her own mum. Running off and leaving her children, even though she loved us to bits. Which I knew that she *did*.

"Ruby?" Sammy was tugging at me. "What's this?"

"Oh!" Sammy had found a book. A young child's book, with a picture on the cover showing a big yellow sun amongst puffy clouds in a bright blue sky. Birds were flitting to and fro, carrying bits of leaf and twig. A squirrel sat at the foot of a tree, munching an acorn. Flowers, all colours of the rainbow, poked through grass that was emerald green.

Sammy sat staring at it, entranced. "Pretty!" she said.

I agreed that it was. I would have loved it when I was Sammy's age. Mum must have loved it, too, cos it was quite tattered and torn. It had obviously been read A LOT.

I opened it – and immediately rocked back on my heels. There, on the very first page, the words leapt out at me: Lemonade Sky.

In a lemonade sky
Where the clouds hang high
Go dream your dream
Of Hush-a-bye.

"What's it mean?" said Sammy.
"It's poetry," I said.

"But what's it *mean?*"

"It's just words. It's like you said, it's pretty."

"But what does it—"

"I don't know!" I didn't care what it meant. It had been important to Mum, that was all that mattered. My heart was racing. I could hardly wait for Gran to come back!

The minute I heard the car in the driveway I went rushing out, waving the book.

"Gran, Gran, look what I've—"

That was as far as I got before Tizz's voice came clattering at me.

"Guess what? I went for a ride and I didn't fall off once! Gran says I'm a natural."

"You are," said Gran, "but there's no need to boast about it. Other people need a bit of space. What's that you've found, Ruby? Something from your mother's box?"

"Look!" I thrust the book at her. "Lemonade sky!"

"Oh, my goodness." Gran had gone quite pale. "I had no idea." Her hand shook slightly as she turned the pages.

"I'd completely forgotten about it. This," she told us, "was your mum's favourite book when she was little. She used to sit on her dad's lap while he read it to her. Over and over… she couldn't get enough of it! I honestly think that was the happiest time of her life. She and her dad were so close. She was a different child after he died. Looking back—" Gran paused, as if momentarily lost in thought. She sighed. "I don't think she ever really got over it."

There was a long silence, while Gran stood there, staring down at the book.

"No idea," she whispered. "I had no idea!"

For once, not even Tizz was brave enough to say anything. It was me, in the end, who asked the question.

"So when Mum said we'd have lemonade sky…"

"She must have been back in her mind all those years ago, when she was just a little girl."

"When she was happy," I said.

"Yes. When she was happy."

"She still *is* happy," said Tizz. "Most of the time, she is."

"It's true," I said. "We have lots of fun! It's only when she gets depressed-"

"When she doesn't take her meds."

"Well." Gran cleared her throat. "In future we must make very sure that she does. I shall have a word with her! And this time," said Gran, "I don't intend to take no for an answer."

CHAPTER TWELVE

That very same evening, Cal rang to say that Mum had come back. It was Gran who took the call and came to give us the news. I immediately grabbed hold of Sammy and began dancing her round the room.

"Mum's back, Mum's back! Now we can go home!"

But oh, it seemed that we couldn't. It wasn't as simple as that. Gran said that now the police were involved, and the Social Services, Mum wouldn't be allowed to have us back until she was judged fit to take care of us.

I waited for Tizz to explode. We'd said all along that Mum would come home. We'd said we shouldn't involve the police. *Now* look what had happened! But Tizz remained silent. I was the one who asked Gran why Mum hadn't rung us herself, and whether we could speak to her.

Quite gently, Gran said that just at the moment she didn't think Mum was in any state to talk to us.

"She's been off her medication for too long."

"Is she depressed?" I said. It was like last time all over again, when Mum had to go into hospital. Oh, and it had been such a horrid hospital! Really scary. Me and Tizz had hated having to visit her there. She hadn't seemed like our mum; more like some total stranger.

"Where has she been?" Tizz put the question, abruptly.

"As far as I can make out," said Gran, "she's been with that friend of hers, Nikki."

"Oh. *Her*," said Tizz. Her lip curled.

"Her and her boyfriend. Apparently they met some —" Gran paused — "some *person* in a club and all went gallivanting off to France together."

"Mum's been in *France*?" I said.

"So it would seem. They'd most likely be there even now if this Nikki hadn't got frightened and brought your mother back home."

"I hate Nikki," I said. "I hate her! She knows Mum's bipolar."

Tizz, rather bitterly, said "What did she think was going to happen to *us*?"

"I don't imagine she thought anything," said Gran. "She sounds like exactly the wrong sort of friend for someone as fragile as your mother. All one can say is at least she brought her back and didn't just abandon her, which she well might have done."

"Cal wouldn't have," I said. Not however much his feet were itching.

"Cal wouldn't have let Mum go running off in the first place," said Tizz.

"No, I'm inclined to think he wouldn't," agreed Gran. "He may be a bit of a drifter, but his heart's obviously in the right place."

I liked the thought of Cal's heart being in the right place. I liked it that Gran approved of him, especially as I had the feeling he wasn't really her kind of person. I said that Mum had always been better when Cal was around.

"He sort of keeps her steady."

"When he's there," said Tizz.

"This is the problem," said Gran. "Your mother certainly needs a steadying influence, but it would take a very special person to saddle himself with such a responsibility."

"Cal *is* a very special person," I said.

Gran didn't deny it; but when I hopefully suggested

that maybe we could all go home and live with Cal until Mum was allowed out of hospital, she said she didn't think that was such a good idea.

"He's not your father, so I doubt Social Services would allow it. I'm afraid you'll have to make do with me for a while. Is that so very bad?"

I had to say no, cos what else could I do? It would have been rude to say I would rather be with Cal.

Gran said, "That's settled, then." She didn't sound as if she minded too much. She seemed to have got used to us and what she called our odd ways. "You can spend the rest of the summer with me and we shall at last get to know one another."

It's the end of August, now. We've been living with Gran for nearly two months. Once a week Gran takes us to visit Mum. She's getting so much better! She's not depressed any more. We go for walks in the hospital grounds, and we tell her everything that's going on in our lives, like how Tizz is learning to ride and how

Gran says she's a natural. I reckon Tizz must have told Mum this about ten times. But I forgive her cos she's also told Mum how I took charge while Mum was away.

"Honestly, she was so bossy you wouldn't believe! All she did all the time was nag at us. But it was probably just as well," said Tizz, "cos otherwise we'd have spent all our money on crisps and stuff, and stayed up all night watching telly, and never gone to school or washed our hair or had a bath or *anything*. It was only thanks to Ruby."

Mum gave me a big hug when Tizz told her this. And when she heard about Sammy washing her own hair, she laughed and said, "I bet there was water everywhere!"

That's when I knew she was getting better, when she started laughing again.

The hospital is quite close, just half an hour away. I *think* Gran might be paying for it. I'm not quite sure, but it's as different as can be from the other place Mum was in. For a start, it's called a clinic rather than a hospital. Secondly, it's a whole lot smaller.

Thirdly, it isn't anywhere near so scary. Not really scary at all.

I was worried the first few times that Gran would start lecturing Mum and that Mum would explode, but I have come to the conclusion that she and Gran really do love each other, in spite of Mum telling Gran to get out of her life. Gran knows she didn't mean it. It was just the bipolar talking. At any rate, Gran hasn't lectured and Mum hasn't exploded.

I'm hoping that by September Mum will be able to leave the clinic and we can all go back home. Otherwise, what would happen about school? I don't want to have to start at a new one. I wrote to Nina and told her I would be coming back, and now that Gran has given us our own email addresses we send each other emails all the time. I would hate not to see her again! But I think it will be all right, cos last time we visited Mum she was really bright and chirpy. She said, "Darlings, I'm going to turn over a new leaf! In future I'm going to take my tablets *every single day*. I promise!"

Tizz said, "Mum, we've heard that before."

Mum said, "Yes, but this time I mean it!"

I thought to myself that if Cal were still with us he would make sure Mum kept her promise. If only his feet didn't start itching again! If they did, it would have to be up to me. But I wouldn't mind! Just as long as were all together.

It's not so terribly bad, living with Gran. I do enjoy having a garden to play in, and I've started learning the names of all the birds that visit us. The only ones I could ever recognise before were sparrows and pigeons. Oh, and seagulls, of course, from the docks. Maybe robins, though I never actually saw one. Only on Christmas cards. Now I can recognize blackbirds and thrushes and bluetits and swallows, and all the tiny little finches that flit about amongst the bushes making their high-pitched chittering sounds. Sammy likes to put food out for them. She very proudly fills up their nut bags and changes the water in the bird bath. We have even become friends with Piper, who is quite a nice dog once you get to know him. He is going to miss us when we go home, especially Tizz. They are always together. He has even started sleeping on her bed.

I think I might miss Gran; just a little bit. She is rather strict, and insists that we tidy up after ourselves and always clear things away after every meal and not just let stuff pile up in the sink like we did at home. If we make any kind of mess, like dropping crumbs on the carpet, she expects us to use the dustpan and brush and sweep them up *immediately*. If we have a bath, we have to clean the bath afterwards, a thing I never heard of!

It is funny that her house is so clean and neat while her stables are so messy. All that hay all over the place, and all the mud brought in on people's boots. It seems messy to me, though maybe, for a stables, it is quite normal. Me and Sammy don't very often go there. We're not really horsey people. Tizz is there practically every day, doing what she calls 'mucking out', which means cleaning up after the horses have done things, then giving them fresh bedding so that they can do some more. Yuck! Not for me. But Tizz absolutely loves it.

I sometimes wonder about Tizz. Me and Sammy can't wait to get back home, but Tizz… I am not so sure. I pointed out to her, the other day, that she could always come and stay with Gran in school holidays. She said, "I suppose. But it wouldn't be the same!"

What was she saying? That she didn't want to come home?

"Know what would be really good?" said Tizz. "If we could live here all the time."

Rather shocked, I said, "Without Mum?"

"No! Of course not without Mum. Mum could come and live here as well. Then we could all be together and wouldn't have to go back to South Street."

"But that's our home," I said.

"But this is nicer," said Tizz.

I don't know. I'm not sure Gran would want that.

Even though they love each other, I can't see her and Mum managing to live together.

"Anyway," said Tizz. "That's what I reckon ought to happen. I suppose you'd rather just go back to the way things were before."

"Not quite," I said.

There's this one big difference. I didn't tell Tizz, but I have a secret dream. I dream that Cal's feet will finally stop itching and that he will never go away from us, ever again. I even dream that he and Mum will get married, and that we can be a real proper family.

Lemonade sky, my darlings! We'll all have lemonade sky!

Of course I know that it *is* only a dream. But who said dreams can't come true? Dreams come true all the time. You just have to dream as hard as you can…

More fantastic reads from Jean Ure...

ICE LOLLY

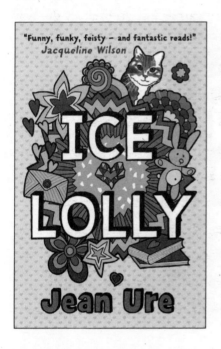

Without Mum, everything is just so *hard*. Things would be easier if I could just stop feeling; if I could just freeze, like an ice lolly...

More fantastic reads from Jean Ure...

SKINNY MELON AND ME

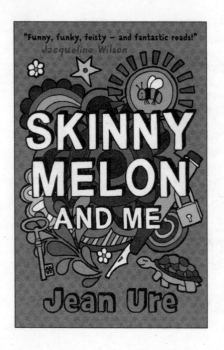

This is the diary of Cherry Louise Waterton. Problem One: My mum's just remarried a total dweeb named Roland Butter. Problem Two: I think she also has a secret too...